"I—" Words
stammered

"Hi. I hope you don't mind me dropping by." The deep, husky voice had its usual effect, setting the blood racing in her veins and bringing a tight knot of desire to her stomach.

"No. No, of course not." Alex felt ridiculously flustered and uncertain. "What can I do for you?"

Kyle regarded her for a few moments in silence, as if trying himself to remember why he had come. Sighing, he ran the fingers of one hand through his hair, dislodging a couple of wayward locks, which fell across his forehead.

"I wondered… Hell, Alexandra, I don't really know. I just needed to talk," he admitted. There was such confusion and loneliness in his voice that her heart melted, and it was all she could do not to fling her arms around him and hug him tight.

Dear Reader,

I have a very soft spot in my heart for gorgeous but troubled Kyle Sinclair—a caring doctor and a good man, but one who has been through the emotional mill in the past couple of years. I was determined to find him a strong and independent woman with a heart of gold. A woman who would see the man he is inside, and who would help him to live and trust and love again. I discovered that woman in Alexandra Patterson, a dedicated, caring nurse who has known loss and disappointment herself.

This is the third linked book set in fictional general practitioners' offices in close-knit rural communities in beautiful southwest Scotland. It is tough to say goodbye to characters I have come to know so well, but you never know—news of them could turn up in future stories. I may not be able to resist it! It has been lovely catching up with Nic and Hannah and Conor and Kate again, but I hope you will now enjoy the emotional journey Kyle and Alexandra must travel, and that you come to love them as much as I do.

Thank you for your support and interest.

Happy reading,

Margaret McDonagh

His Very Special Nurse

Margaret McDonagh

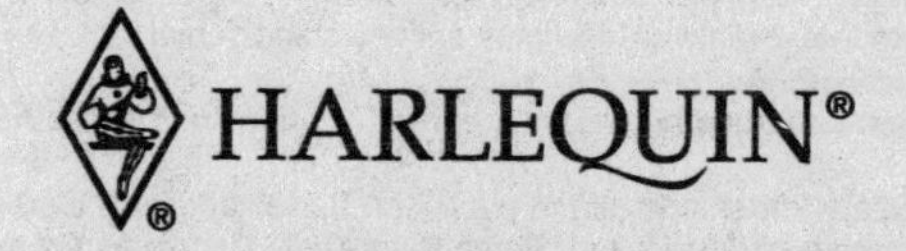

TORONTO • NEW YORK • LONDON
AMSTERDAM • PARIS • SYDNEY • HAMBURG
STOCKHOLM • ATHENS • TOKYO • MILAN • MADRID
PRAGUE • WARSAW • BUDAPEST • AUCKLAND

ISBN-13: 978-0-373-06614-8
ISBN-10: 0-373-06614-7

HIS VERY SPECIAL NURSE

First North American Publication 2007

This edition published by arrangement with Harlequin Books S.A.

www.eHarlequin.com

Printed in U.S.A.

His Very Special Nurse

For Jackie, Lesley, Christine and Irene,
the best district nurses in the world…
thank you for all your kindness and care.

And with thanks to Joanne and Sheila for all their
support and encouragement.

CHAPTER ONE

'I HAVE a proposition for you, Alexandra.'

Alex Patterson swallowed. The man's voice sent shivers of awareness along her spine, and the way he spoke her name raised the hairs on the back of her neck. Deeper than one would expect from looking at him, his voice had an attractive Scottish burr, and sounded like honey drizzling through gravel: rough, husky and temptingly moreish. The kind of voice that should be employed on TV commercials, enticing people to buy things they didn't need. Her grey gaze met a sultry, midnight-blue one and heat seared through her entire body. She could feel her pulse throbbing in her neck and was grateful to take the chair he indicated, her legs decidedly shaky. The only proposition she could imagine a man like him making was one she should definitely say no to—the kind that would lead a good girl wickedly astray and turn her thoughts to sin. Excitement rippled through her, and she fought the urge to wipe suddenly damp palms on her smart trousers. Hannah hadn't warned her that Dr Kyle Sinclair was seriously sexy. A fantasy bad boy come to life.

'A proposition?' she managed, hoping her voice sounded considerably cooler and more composed than she felt.

As Kyle closed the door and moved round the table in the

small meeting room to sit down, Alex continued her assessment of his athletic build…six feet of lean muscle encased in a charcoal suit, the crisp whiteness of his shirt highlighting his bronzed skin. In his early thirties, she judged, his dark hair was short and thick, the couple of stray locks that flopped onto his forehead failing to soften the brooding expression on his far-too-handsome face. The Fates had been more than generous when handing out Kyle's looks. He was enough to turn any woman's head and make her forget every scrap of common sense she possessed. A faint dark shadow edged the lean masculinity of his stubborn jaw, and she heard the light rasp as he ran the palm of one hand over his stubbled chin. As for his mouth… Unable to help it, Alex's gaze lingered there. It was a sensuous mouth, tempting, full of dark promise, the Cupid's bow that shaped his top lip matched with the fullness of his lower one, giving him a sexy pout that was sinfully distracting.

Aware she was staring, Alex shifted her focus, only to find their gazes locking and holding once more. A fresh wave of heat coursed through her veins. It was hard to decipher the expression in those inscrutable cobalt eyes, impossible to read what he was thinking. She couldn't explain why, but she had the impression this man was not as he seemed—smooth and efficient on the outside, but full of contradictions, guarding hidden emotions inside. Troubled, hurt, alone. A shiver rippled through her, part awareness, part unease. He lowered his hand from his face and opened the file in front of him before looking up to speak.

'My understanding is that you are seeking a full-time position as a district nurse.' Alex nodded when he paused, endeavouring to concentrate on the reason for this meeting, needing to re-establish a sense of purpose and ignore the man's appeal. 'Unfortunately, we don't have such a position available.'

Disappointment clutched at her and she shifted on her chair, wondering why the information could not have been relayed over the phone, saving them both this charade. 'Then I won't take up any more of your valuable time.' Trying to hide how deflated she was, she reached for her bag and began to stand.

'However…'

Pausing, she glanced up, her throat closing as she looked at him. 'Yes?'

'It was suggested that I talk with you first and then, if you are interested, the other partners will meet with us for a more formal discussion.'

'I see.' She didn't see at all, but she was struggling to maintain her composure. Something about being in this man's presence was managing to fry her brain and disturb her usual calm. Subsiding back on the chair, she set her bag down again and drew in a shaky breath. 'What do you wish to talk about?'

Steepling his hands, he watched her, the frown making him appear even more serious and unapproachable. 'I've studied your CV, and noted you have experience not only as a district nurse but working within a practice surgery as well.'

'That is correct.' Her own hands clenched in her lap as she forced herself to meet and match his expressionless regard. When he glanced away, releasing her from that magnetic dark-blue spell, she sucked air into parched lungs. 'Although I worked within a hospital for some time first.'

'In Edinburgh.'

'Yes. I did my training there, and stayed on the wards for some time before going to work in general practice.'

'And then you relocated to the south of England?'

Alex nodded, unwilling to divulge the personal reasons for her move and the change of direction in her career. 'I did some agency nursing for practices at first, and then progressed to the District Nurse Specialist Practitioner Programme.'

'Why district nursing?'

'I enjoy following through with patients,' she explained, more confident now she was on surer ground, sincere about her work. 'The ongoing care is important to me, rather than just shipping people out of the ward and not knowing what happens to them.'

'You believe in holistic care?' Kyle questioned, nothing in his tone indicating whether he approved or disapproved of her views.

Once more she made the mistake of looking at him, and fought the fierce inner response that rushed through her the second eye contact was established. She struggled to focus on what she wanted to say. 'Very much so. To me it's about caring for the whole person, knowing them and their situation, their carers and families, working as much for prevention as cure, being there to help and advise.'

'Mmm.'

Alex was unsure whether the brief lift of his brow indicated agreement or whether he was mocking her. Silence stretched, and, nervous, she was compelled to break it. 'Is there some other vacancy available here, Dr Sinclair?' she pressed, eager to bring this torturous interview to a conclusion.

'What we have are two part-time vacancies. We've been using agency nurses to cover both positions, but it is not satisfactory on a long term basis.' He paused a moment, leaning forward and pushing the file containing her CV aside before folding his arms on the table. 'It isn't something we had considered before, but with your combined experience and qualifications we thought it might work. How would you feel about taking on both roles? It would add up to the full-time hours you are seeking but would mean some days spent working here in the surgery and some days as a district nurse out in the community.'

The suggestion took Alex by surprise. It was an unusual arrangement, but one that had definite appeal. She desperately wanted to remain in this area of rural south-west Scotland where she had grown up, and to be able to maintain the family home her father had left to her, but to do so she needed a full-time job. Badly. Local vacancies for the work she desired had proved elusive, and although if worst came to worst she could try the district hospital in the main county town, she really didn't want to go back on the wards. Kyle's notion of her taking on the dual roles at the Glenside Surgery in Rigtownbrae could be the answer to her prayers.

'Yes,' she allowed, her decision made. 'I would be interested in doubling up—should you and your partners decide I am suitable.'

Alex suppressed a tingle as Kyle took a moment to survey her once more, his slow inspection tightening her insides and speeding up her already racing pulse. 'It would mean some juggling with the rotas and maybe some irregular shifts. The district nurses have a working arrangement with other local practices for out-of-hours work, so you will have occasional weekend duties.'

'That won't be a problem. I'll be happy to fit in as needed.' Alex tried a smile, her nerves refusing to abate despite the more hopeful outcome that might lie ahead. 'May I ask, what out-of-hours cover the practice works as far as the doctors are concerned?'

'The majority vote was to switch to the deputizing service.' Kyle's jaw tightened, and she guessed the subject had been a bone of contention between the partners. Alex tried to prevent her feelings from showing. No doubt as a young doctor Kyle wanted his evenings and weekends free for his social life. It was a common trend now, but one she disapproved of. 'It's no secret that I wasn't keen on the idea,' he continued, the edge in his voice surprising her as much as his words. 'I believe we should have followed Lochanrig's example in maintaining our own service. The patients aren't keen on the new system—and it's all about that continuity of care you were talking about, not just fobbing them off with whoever is available, someone who doesn't know anything about them or their histories.'

Alex held her tongue, glancing at Kyle from under her lashes, rethinking her opinion of him, impressed by his words and the sincerity in his voice. She knew first hand about the special care provided by the neighbouring practice he had mentioned. Her father had been registered with Lochanrig, founded and maintained by the Frost family, and she would always be grateful for the wonderful attention he had received from Drs Hannah Frost and Nic Di Angelis, the married couple who'd run the practice since Hannah's parents had died.

Alex had come to know them and their team of nurses well over the last year or more. Some of the staff she remembered from her youth, while dedicated, generous Hannah and her attractive Italian husband had become welcome friends. Throughout his illness, her father would have hated some stranger attending him if there was a problem, but fortunately either Nic or Hannah had always been on hand, especially near the end. It had made a big difference to her father and herself to have the continuity of care that Kyle clearly championed as much as she did. However much he was unsettling her on a personal level, that he felt so strongly about the issue pleased her, because it had to mean he cared about his patients.

Her father had lost his long battle against his illness two months ago and, having put her career and her life on hold for more than a year to care for him, Alex knew it was time to venture onward again, no matter how difficult, and how much she still felt the painful loss. There were no vacancies at Lochanrig but everyone had encouraged her to stay local, to follow her dream to keep the family home going, and to revive her career here. It was Hannah who had tipped her off about the possible vacancy in Rigtownbrae, who had encouraged her to send her CV, and who had arranged for her to meet Kyle Sinclair.

Maybe this part district nursing, part working at the surgery role was just what she needed to step back into life again. Although how she would feel having Kyle as a colleague she couldn't imagine. Hannah and Nic hadn't told her much about their friend, but Kyle was not what she had expected, and clearly he was not an easy man to know or understand. He had a restless edge, as if something was simmering inside him, and she sensed all was not well in his life, that he had been hurt somehow—and that hurt was festering. Maybe she recognised it because she shared it, was still grieving for her much-loved father…and for the life she had willingly but suddenly left behind to come home and nurse him.

As Kyle flicked through the papers in the file once more, the perpetual frown knotting his brow, Alex bit back a sigh. Her palms still felt clammy, and the butterflies were still conducting acrobatic manoeuvres in her stomach. She didn't remember ever being this nervous, not because she doubted her qualifications or abilities, but because this meant so much to her and she wanted, *needed,* this job. It didn't help that she was so conscious of Kyle Sinclair and his sinful attractiveness. He made her anxious, uncertain, flustered. She might be ready to get back to work, but she wasn't sure she could handle the thought of being interested in a man again. Not that she was interested in Kyle, she hastened to reassure herself, but her reaction to him had given her a jolt.

It had been a long time since she had even noticed a man. Not since Mitchell. She covered the exclamation that fought to escape by turning the sound into a smothered cough. Now was not the time to think of Mitchell. They had been together for over two years. She had left Scotland and proximity to her father to move down to the south of England to be with him, because of his need to further his career. She had loved him, had believed he felt the same, had trusted him, agreed to marry him, had thought she knew all there was to know about him. Yet it turned out she hadn't really known him at all. The sense of betrayal still hurt. And she would never forget what he had done, or the words he had spoken.

Unsettled by her thoughts, and on edge at the continuing silence, she looked at Kyle's bent head, dismayed to find herself wondering if his dark hair would feel as silken to the touch as it looked. Alarmed, she dragged her gaze away and stared out of the window, feeling that if he didn't speak soon she was going to explode! Just as he snapped the file closed and returned his attention to her, Alex's mouth opened in shock as she saw an elderly man, who was passing on the pavement across the road from the surgery stumble a moment and then crash to the ground.

'Alexandra, I—'

'Oh my goodness!'

'Excuse me?'

Unmindful of where she was and how important this appointment could be to her future, she thrust back her chair and hurried from the room, blind to the dumbstruck expression on Kyle Sinclair's face.

'What the hell?'

Bemused, Kyle watched the door bounce back on its hinges as the woman disappeared from view down the corridor. Her bag remained on the table, either left behind in her inexplicable urge to flee, or because she intended to return, he had no idea which. But, then, he had long ago given up trying to understand women. What had just happened to drive cool, composed Alexandra Patterson to urgent action? She'd been looking past him out of the window, he realised, turning to gaze at the rain-washed scene outside. His eyes widened as he saw her dash across the road in front of an oncoming car and fall to her knees on the opposite pavement, beside the prone figure of crusty old Joe Harmon. Swearing under his breath, Kyle sped from his own chair, grabbed some supplies from his consulting room and rushed through Reception, leaving startled staff and patients in his wake.

By the time he joined Alexandra, she'd taken off her jacket, seemingly impervious to the wet, windy autumn afternoon, and she used it to shelter the man's balding, bloodied head from the worst of the rain. Handing her a pair of surgical gloves, Kyle pulled on his own and forced his attention away from the distracting sight of the increasingly wet shirt clinging to Alexandra's generous, feminine curves. It was more than time he focused on their patient.

'What have you been up to, Joe?' he asked, carrying out a swift but detailed assessment of the pensioner's injuries, checking for any neck trauma, receiving only a surly grunt in reply.

'He tripped.' Kyle glanced up at Alexandra's intervention, startled anew by her smoky grey eyes. 'From what I saw, he caught his foot on a paving slab and went right over, banging his head. He seems to have damaged his shoulder and he has a graze on his hand, too.'

Kyle frowned. He had discovered that. He was the doctor after all. Yet he felt surplus to requirements as Alexandra worked competently on the other side of Joe, stemming the bleeding from the nasty head wound, applying pressure on a pad, and talking soothingly to the disoriented, grumpy man.

'I need to get home,' Joe insisted, struggling to move.

'In a little while,' Alexandra promised. 'You took a nasty tumble. Just let Dr Sinclair check you over, and then we'll help you inside and get you comfortable.'

Knowing how curmudgeonly and uncooperative Joe could be, Kyle's eyes widened in surprise as the old man relaxed and submitted to Alexandra's advice and ministrations. 'Are you feeling dizzy or nauseous?' he asked now, trying to retake control of the situation.

'Bit dizzy.' The admission was grudging.

'Did you feel that way before your fall?'

'No, I was fine. Until I found that there broken stone.'

Kyle looked at the offending piece of pavement and planned to telephone the council. 'Aside from your head, can you tell me where else you are hurting, Joe?'

'My shoulder. It's excruciating,' he admitted, face tight with pain.

'We'll get you comfortable as soon as we can,' Kyle promised. 'Let us do the work, but shout out if something hurts or you need a rest.'

Reassuring himself that there appeared to be no other damage, Kyle accepted Alexandra's silent assistance in helping move Joe into a sitting position, pausing a moment for the man to take a few breaths and get his bearings before trying to help him stand. Practice manager Lisa Sharpe and nurse Sheena Ellis joined them, but Kyle dispatched them back to the surgery to make a place ready for Joe while he and Alexandra slowly walked the pensioner across the road and forecourt before entering the building. Once inside, Joe muttered about the fuss as he was settled in one of the treatment rooms, but he was clearly in considerable discomfort. Alexandra held his hand, talking to him as Sheena set to work cleaning the nasty cut on his head, which would need stitches, and the graze on his other hand, while Kyle focused on assessing the injury to shoulder and arm.

'I'm sorry, Joe, but you're going to need a trip to town to the hospital for an X-ray.' Kyle nodded to Lisa Sharpe who went to the phone to call an ambulance, ignoring Joe's protest. 'There's nothing for it. You've damaged your shoulder, and more than likely there's a break to your collarbone. You've also had a nasty bang to your head, and you need to have that investigated.'

'Can't you fix it here?' Joe pleaded.

Kyle opened his mouth to explain, only to snap it closed again as Alexandra beat him to it. Disgruntled, he folded his arms across his chest and listened to the cadence of her voice, softly accented and gentle as she eased the old man's fears and expertly cajoled him into agreeing to what needed to be done. Sheena, he noted, was clearly impressed and Lisa— Sharpe by name and sharp by nature—had a rare satisfied smile on her face as she studied Alexandra. Meeting his gaze, Lisa gave a determined nod of approval and Kyle's frown deepened.

By the time the ambulance arrived, Joe had been made as comfortable as possible, his head-wound dressed and his arm strapped carefully for the journey to the county town. 'A lot of nonsense,' he grumbled as the paramedics assisted him into the chair and wheeled him out to the waiting vehicle.

Lisa returned to the room with a couple of towels, handing one to Alexandra and one to Kyle so they could dry off. 'I'll make some tea, you must be cold.' Tutting, she bustled away again.

'And I have a spare tunic that should fit you, Alex,' Sheena offered. 'You need to get out of those wet things.'

'Thanks.'

Kyle watched as Alexandra cast a rueful glance over her ruined outfit. Aside from being wet, she had grubby marks on her trousers where she had been kneeling on the pavement, her jacket was creased, dirty and bloodied, and her shirt… He swallowed, closing his eyes and focusing on toweling dry his hair. But the displacement activity did nothing to remove the image of the sheer silvery-grey fabric plastered to Alexandra's torso, revealing the outline of a lacy scrap of black bra encasing her lush breasts. His temper rising, cross with her and himself, Kyle stalked away and returned to the sanctuary of his consulting room, tossing the towel aside and stripping off his wet jacket and shirt, before pulling on a bulky Aran jumper he kept with a change of clothes in one cupboard.

He didn't know why he was so unsettled. He'd been unfocused and on edge since he had met Alexandra Patterson and been closeted with her in the meeting room for the pre-interview discussion. His friends Hannah and Nic, GPs from nearby Lochanrig, had persuaded him to talk to his partners about giving Alexandra the opportunity to fill the dual nursing vacancies they had, vouching for her caring nature and her professional abilities. He knew she had returned to Scotland over a year ago to care for her sick father, dedicating herself to his needs until his recent passing. Now she was ready to return to work. What his friends hadn't said was anything much about Alexandra as a woman. She wasn't what he had expected. Not at all.

At twenty-nine, Alexandra was younger than he had anticipated, and she was distractingly attractive. Her hair, darkly golden like well-ripened corn, was short and thick with a natural wave, and was swept back from a face that while not classically beautiful was instantly arresting. Smoky grey, slightly slanting eyes were framed by impossibly long, sooty lashes under gently arching eyebrows. Then there was the neat nose, the golden, peachy-soft skin and a well-defined jaw that looked as if it could be stubborn if she set her mind on something. But it was her mouth that kept drawing his attention. Kyle closed his eyes at the memory of it, his body tightening in a most unwanted and worrying way. Tempting, irresistible… Her mouth, with its full lower lip and shapely top one, that formed into a kissable pout, was enough to set a fire in his stomach and bring an ache of need he'd not felt in a long time.

He wished he'd never agreed to give Alexandra this interview. She had proved herself skilful and caring with her reactions to old Joe, putting the man's welfare before her own needs in the middle of her appeal for the job. There was little question that his partners would approve of her and she would be offered the dual position at Glenside. Little question that Alexandra would accept. He slumped in his chair, a frown creasing his brow. The last thing he wanted was to see her again, much less have to work with her.

'All right, Kyle?'

Glancing up as the words interrupted his reverie, Kyle nodded at Robert MacKenzie, one of his practice partners. 'Fine.'

'I heard about the excitement.' Warm brown eyes twinkled below the thatch of greying hair. Married to Lindsay, a local teacher, and with two grown children, Robert was approaching sixty. He was already cutting back his work hours and planning his retirement, and discussion was ongoing about appointing a new junior doctor next spring. 'We're waiting in the meeting room to finalise the details of Alex's employment. Join us when you're ready.'

Three hours later, his temper far from improved, Kyle let himself into his soulless house not far from the surgery, dumped his belongings and stalked through to the kitchen, smothering a groan as the telephone rang.

'Sinclair,' he barked into the receiver.

'How did it go?'

Hannah. He should have guessed.

'How did what go?' Kyle prevaricated, wedging the phone between his ear and his shoulder as he surveyed the meagre, unappetising contents of his fridge.

'The interview with Alex.'

Kyle's scowl intensified. The last thing he wanted was to think any more about Alexandra Patterson. 'It was eventful. But she got the job.'

'That's great!' Hannah's smile was evident from her voice. 'Whatever happened, though?'

He thought back to the moment when Alexandra had shot out of her chair, leaving him staring after her in shocked silence. Feeling grumpy, he related the incident to Hannah, pulling a bottle of beer out of the fridge before slamming the door shut.

'I told you Alex was a good nurse,' Hannah chuckled.

'If nothing else it demonstrated her competence,' he allowed reluctantly, unable to banish his deep-seated unease. 'Robert and Elizabeth were impressed and insisted we take her on.'

A moment of silence followed his statement. 'Didn't you want to give Alex the job?'

'I'm not sure combining both roles is a good idea.'

That wasn't the problem, but he wasn't discussing his reservations, his confused feelings, with Hannah. Alexandra unsettled his world, disturbed the very air around him, had done from the second he'd met her. He didn't like it. He didn't want it. They needed her at the surgery but he wasn't going to like working with her, and he planned to avoid her as much as possible.

'And what about you? What did you think about Alex?' Hannah pressed.

'She's well qualified and keen to take on the dual responsibilities.'

'I meant as a person!'

'I've no idea,' he lied, closing his mind to unwanted images of the wretched woman, images that lingered to torment him despite all his efforts to deny them. 'I didn't notice.'

'Oh, Kyle.'

He tensed at the sadness and exasperation in Hannah's voice, his suspicions increasing about why she had set this up and had sent Alexandra to him for the job. Was she just doing a favour for a friend who needed work, or had there been some ulterior motive for pushing Alexandra under his nose? No, Hannah wouldn't do that. Would she? His friends knew how he felt, knew what he'd been through, knew he wasn't interested in any kind of relationship again.

Grateful to hang up the phone a short while later, he opened his beer and carried it through to the living room, where he sat in the dark and brooded on his thoughts. Thoughts that, to his fury, were dominated by Alexandra Patterson. Who did she think she was, coming here, invading his territory, unsettling his peace of mind? He wanted nothing to do with women. They were a menace as a species and, on a personal level, they were off limits for good. Women were trouble. They caused hurt and loss and betrayal. He was having none of it. Not any more. The last eighteen months had been the worst of his life. All due to a woman. His wife.

Ex-wife.

The bitter sting of pain and grief lanced through him. No way was he ever going there again.

Alexandra Patterson could take her smoky grey eyes, pouting lips and curvy body and get the hell out of his head.

CHAPTER TWO

ALEX picked up the receiver, silently cursing the way her fingers trembled as they hovered over the button before pressing it. This was ridiculous. She shouldn't feel as nervous as a breathless teenager with a crush. It wasn't a crush. It wasn't anything. She was just new at Glenside Surgery and finding her way around, anxious to settle into a new routine. Drs Robert MacKenzie and Elizabeth Ross had taken matters out of the hands of a silent, frowning Kyle Sinclair and, impressed with her aiding Joe Harmon—when surely anyone would have done the same having seen the elderly man's crashing fall—had offered her the job. Both jobs. Which Alex had accepted, thankful and determined, only now to find herself as jittery as a novice. Because she wanted to prove herself, that was all. Reassured by her silent pep talk, she cast hesitation aside and stabbed the extension key on the phone with more force than necessary, waiting for the connection to be made.

'Sinclair.'

Of course proving herself professionally was all it was, an irritating voice mocked in her head. That's why you've gone all fluttery and unnecessary, just having the man bark his surname in your ear. She struggled to keep all emotion and anxiety from her own tone. 'Dr Sinclair, it's Nurse Patterson.

I have Mrs Parkin with me in Treatment Room One. There's a note on her file asking that you be informed of her visit. Do you wish to make an examination before I re-dress her wound?'

'Yes, I do. Thanks. I'll be there in a moment.'

Her hand was *not* trembling when she set down the receiver following his abrupt and impersonal reply. She was perfectly fine. And she would behave in a perfectly calm and efficient way when Kyle arrived, just as she had been doing all through her first week in her new split-role job. He only made her nervous because he was so brooding and intimidating. It had nothing at all to do with the fact that he was the most mysterious, gorgeous, sinfully sexy man she had ever encountered, and that every time she saw him or heard his deeply rough voice he took her breath away. Nothing whatever. Pulling herself together, she returned to the treatment table and took Cathy Parkin's warm, plump hand in hers, knowing how nervous the lady was.

'Dr Sinclair will be here shortly,' she informed her, relieved that her voice sounded calm and collected, betraying none of the turmoil roiling inside her.

'I'm glad it's him, dear.' The rotund, middle-aged woman managed a tremulous smile. 'He's always kind. I probably shouldn't say this, but Dr Ross doesn't have the same bedside manner.'

Unwilling to discuss the three GP partners, Alex smiled her reassurance and chatted to ex-librarian Cathy about books, putting her at ease while they waited for Kyle. Her own thoughts strayed, however. For all his reserve and brooding intensity, she had discovered Kyle was infinitely calm and genuinely caring with his patients. Robert MacKenzie was like everyone's benevolent if slightly absent-minded grandfather, but it was true she had found Elizabeth Ross—a brisk, fiercely efficient woman in her forties—to be clinically excellent but somewhat lacking in people skills. However, she had not been at the practice a full week yet and was loathe to make hasty judgements about her new colleagues, much less discuss them with patients.

Everyone had been welcoming and had gone out of their way to help her fit in. With the exception of Penny Collins, one of the district nurses. The few times their paths had crossed, the woman had been viciously unpleasant. Not that Penny had spoken a word. She didn't have to. The venomous looks she flung at her at every opportunity spoke volumes, but Alex had yet to discover what she had done to cause such a reaction from someone she had never met before.

Kyle was the only other person whose welcome had been far from warm, she admitted, her brow furrowing at the thought. He had been polite, professional but distant, which given her unwarranted and unwelcome reaction to his presence was probably a good thing—even though his cautious, wary manner brought a pang of regret she had no business feeling. It was ironic that after over a year of hibernation and abstinence the first man she should find attractive and be unable to stop thinking about was out of bounds, far too complex to understand, and not the least bit interested in her. Which didn't prevent her heart leaping in her chest when a knock at the door preceded his arrival and the man in question stepped into the room, making it seem smaller, and sucking most of the available oxygen out of the atmosphere. This was crazy.

For a moment their gazes locked and Alex fought her reaction, deliberately returning her attention to Cathy Parkin, and moving to the other side of the treatment table to allow Kyle room to assess the woman's ulcerated leg.

'Hello, Cathy, good to see you again.' Kyle took the hand Alex had so recently been holding, his bedside manner exemplary. 'How have you been?'

'Not too bad, doctor. I don't mind telling you, though, that

I'm a tad fed up with this wretched leg,' she muttered, her worried brown gaze fixed on Kyle's face.

With a final squeeze of her hand, Kyle nodded. 'I'm sure you are. Let's take a look, shall we? It certainly seems less red, hot and tender than before, even if the surface area of the ulcer hasn't shrunk as swiftly as I would have liked,' he allowed, concentrating on his task.

As she listened to him talk, Alex watched him, noting how the smile for his patient failed to strip the aloneness and inner hurt from his eyes. He devoted all his attention to Cathy, his mouth a sensual pout, and Alex couldn't help but wonder what those lips would feel like on hers, how he would taste. A couple of errant curls flopped onto his forehead, and her fingers itched to brush them back, to sink into the thickness of his rakish dark hair. No doubt about it, Kyle was stunning to look at, but all that smouldering sexuality and latent masculinity had never appealed to her before. Why now? No matter how much she told herself that Kyle was not her type, that she wasn't interested—and neither was he—she couldn't put him out of her mind. Nor could she ignore the frisson of awareness that prickled along her spine when she was with him. She wished she understood why he was so reserved and distant, what had put those painful shadows in his eyes, but although she had only known him a very short time she guessed he wasn't a man given to sharing confidences. Hannah had hinted at some trouble in Kyle's life, but Alex had yet to discover what precisely had happened to him. For now, she struggled to ignore his presence and concentrate on what was being discussed about Mrs Parkin.

'How are Cathy's arterial pulses?' Kyle asked, and Alex snapped back into professional mode, setting her concerns about him aside...at least temporarily.

'The ankle brachial pressures are fine, as is capillary return, and the foot is warm.'

Kyle nodded, checking the notes. 'The most recent swab showed no sign of abnormal bacteria or infection, so I'm not going to prescribe any more antibiotics. Have you been keeping your leg elevated as much as possible, Cathy? What about the smoking?'

'I've not had a cigarette for over two months,' the woman confirmed with a shy but proud smile.

'Well done! And are you sticking to the low-fat diet?'

'I am.' A faint tinge of colour stained her plump cheeks. 'Most of the time. I confess to one or two small lapses.'

Smiling again, Kyle squeezed her fingers. 'Do the best you can. We'll give you all the support you need.'

Alex knew that smoking was one of several factors which could affect chronic venous insufficiency, and Cathy being on the heavy side didn't help either. At least there was no sign of diabetes, she acknowledged, before Kyle reclaimed her attention with his instructions.

'We'll continue with the four-layer compression bandaging, please, Alexandra.'

'Of course, doctor,' she agreed politely, noting the way he insisted on using her full name, as if it were more formal, keeping a distance between them.

'One of the nurses will see you again in seven days, Cathy, but call if you need us or if you have any wetness on the bandages,' Kyle advised with another smile for the patient. Glancing up, he gave a brief nod before stepping away. 'Thank you.'

To stop herself staring after him, Alex turned to fetch the items she needed, feeling the change in atmosphere, and an easing of her breathing as the door closed behind him. Readying herself, she smiled at Cathy. 'Right, let's set about making you comfortable.'

'Dr Sinclair's lovely, isn't he?' Her patient sighed.

Reluctant to gossip, Alex made a non-committal sound and concentrated on applying a non-adherent dressing to the cleaned site of the ulcer. 'He seems to be a very good doctor.'

'Yes, indeed,' Cathy agreed. 'Such a shame what happened. He hasn't been the same since. It's so sad. He was always such fun, and now he never smiles or laughs as he used to, just dedicates himself to his patients. It was such a shock to everyone when his marriage broke up the way it did. They seemed a contented couple.'

Alex found her mind buzzing at the information as she applied a soft bandage to protect ankle and shin bones. Kyle had been married? Was he divorced? What had happened to leave him so alone and cause those who knew him to be so sad for the man he had become? It seemed Kyle may not have come to terms with the breakdown of his marriage and she wondered, an ache in her heart, if he was still in love with his ex-wife. Alarmed at her thoughts, she concentrated on her task, applying the second layer in the form of a crêpe bandage. Usually she enjoyed bandaging, finding it therapeutic and rewarding, knowing she was bringing comfort to her patient. But today, with the revelations about Kyle, she felt on edge, restless. Frowning, she attended to the third layer, this time using an elasticated bandage to apply compression to the leg before the final layer, a further compression bandage, which also helped keep everything together.

'All finished, Cathy. Does it feel all right for you?'

'Perfect. You've been very kind to me, dear, and so gentle. It's good to see another friendly face around the surgery. I hope I'll be lucky enough to have more of my appointments with you.'

Touched, Alex smiled as she helped Cathy Parkin to her feet and accompanied her out to the waiting area to meet up with her husband. 'Thank you. Don't hesitate to let us know if you need anything.'

'I promise.' The woman gave her hand a gentle pat, before adjusting her walking stick and linking her free arm through her husband's. 'I hope you'll be happy here at Glenside.'

Returning to the treatment room to attend to the remainder of her afternoon list, Alex echoed the sentiment. Her thoughts again turned to Kyle and to the welter of unexpected, inconvenient and confused feelings he inspired in her—and she hoped she had not made a mistake, coming here and taking on this job.

'I have the blood results, John, and I'm afraid there is a significant rise in the prostate-specific antigen level,' Kyle explained, hating the need to break potentially worrying news to his patient about the PSA test.

John Archibald, a local solicitor in his late fifties, nodded with resignation. 'Both my father and my uncle had prostate disease. Because of that I have always been aware what can happen.'

'Have you been noticing other signs?'

'I've had some discomfort, plus there are more nights when I need to use the bathroom, and I'm experiencing an increasing urgency to go…with some hesitation when I do.'

'You can have difficulty passing urine because the prostate swells and puts pressure on the urethra,' Kyle explained, making notes as John outlined his symptoms.

'I knew it was best to see you right away.'

Prostate cancer was one of the commonest forms of cancer in men but John had presented early, and Kyle hoped that if he did have the disease they had caught it before it had spread. 'Your symptoms don't necessarily mean it *is* cancer, but it is always best to be cautious, especially with your family history.'

'So what will happen now?'

'I'll be referring you to the urologist.'

'Surgery?'

'Not necessarily.' Despite the man's calm intelligence, Kyle knew he was anxious. 'The urologist will be able to give you much clearer guidance when he's done his own assessment. He'll do more tests, an ultrasound, and a biopsy if required, then he can discuss with you what is the best course of action.'

John was silent for a moment. 'I know there can be problems after surgery.'

'There can be, in some cases, but it depends on so many factors. Let's take this a step at a time, and between us we'll deal with any issues if and when they happen.'

'You're right. I'm getting ahead of myself,' John admitted with a rueful smile. 'Thanks, Doc.'

'No problem. I'll make that referral immediately but contact me at any time if there is anything you want to ask or you notice any change in your symptoms.'

'I will. Thank you.'

After John Archibald had gone, and with his consultations over for the day, Kyle finished writing up the notes and made the request for a referral before leaning back in his chair with a sigh. He felt more weary than usual at the end of a busy week and, loath as he was to admit it, he suspected his edgy tiredness was as much due to the unsettling and disturbing presence of Alexandra Patterson as to his hectic work schedule. His brow knotted in a frown. What was it about the woman that made him so jumpy, so aware? Whatever it was, he didn't want the feelings. He wanted them—and her—to go away. Thankfully he was out of the surgery until Monday, and tomorrow he was meeting up with his best friend, Conor Anderson, a GP at the rural practice in Glentown-on-Firth some miles west. Together they were joining Nic di Angelis in Lochanrig and spending the day walking out on the hills. The wide open spaces and the company of those he trusted always helped soothe his battered spirit, and he certainly felt in need of soothing after the jumble of unwanted feelings that had been churning inside him since meeting Alexandra.

The last eighteen months had been hellish. Who would have thought things could change so drastically in that time? One moment his life had been ordered, settled and content, the future lying ahead as planned, full of hope and promise—but then everything had unravelled around him. He had struggled to hold things together, but whatever he had done had seemed wrong and he had only made things worse. What had happened? How had everything gone so bad so quickly? Remembering didn't seem to become any easier, and nothing eased the grief…nor the heavy weight of his guilt. He scrubbed his hands over his face, trying to shut it out, make it go away, praying for some kind of absolution he knew he didn't deserve. Sometimes he felt as if he was struggling through quicksand, using up all his energy but unable to make any progress, held back from some unknown destination…a place he needed to reach but could never identify.

He had shut himself off emotionally, closed himself down, and he had never wavered in his determination to remain alone from now on, to guard his feelings. To concentrate all his energies on his work, spending his limited free time on his hobbies and doing extra shifts as a BASICS doctor, on call to attend local accidents or emergencies. He only had room in his life for his small circle of trusted friends. No one else was allowed close. So why had one glimpse of Alexandra started to awaken feelings he believed had frozen for ever? Why did the feelings get stronger every day, confusing and disturbing him, each moment with her becoming more of a test to his resolve, his very belief about what was best for him? He didn't want to be awakened, thawed. He resented it. And he resented her for making it happen. He didn't need

Alexandra. He didn't need anyone. Most importantly, he didn't deserve anyone. There was nothing left of himself to give, and he certainly didn't see anything within himself that anyone else could love. Not now.

'You look grim.'

Kyle glanced up and saw district nurse Penny Collins leaning against the door of his consulting room, her uniform tunic and trousers tightly fitted to her petite frame, arms folded as she watched him. 'Just thinking.'

'You do far too much of that,' she berated as she straightened and moved into the room. 'As I keep telling you. And you've been more distracted lately. What's wrong now?'

'Nothing. I was concerned about a patient.' It was a prevarication, but her impatient jibe had stung. He knew he had been more serious and brooding these last months but he felt as if all his insides had been painfully scraped out of him, leaving behind just a shell of the person he had once been.

'Busy day?'

'Aren't they always?' He tried to soften the words with a semblance of a smile. It wasn't Penny's fault he was so cranky. 'At least it's the weekend.'

Pale blue eyes regarded him thoughtfully and with a hint of calculation. 'I'm off this weekend. Want to do something?'

'Thanks, but I have plans. I'm out with Conor and Nic tomorrow, and I have BASICS duty on Sunday.' Grateful for the excuse, he noted how Penny tossed her long braid over her shoulder, a gesture he knew indicated her displeasure.

Penny had been a loyal colleague since his problems had begun, always there with advice and willing to offer help, bringing him food when he wouldn't have eaten. Maybe he'd taken too much advantage of that, or she had read more into it. She had been kind to him, protective when he had felt most vulnerable, although he didn't view her in the same category as Conor, Nic and their wives—the four people closest to him and whom he most trusted.

'Don't worry about me.' He rose to his feet, drawing on his jacket, ready to head for home. 'I'm sure you have some hot date lined up.'

Something flared briefly in her eyes at his teasing, then it was gone and she sent him a cool smile. 'You know me so well.'

As she turned towards the door, he picked up his things and went to follow her, anxious to get home.

'Ouch!'

Kyle halted at Penny's exclamation. 'What's the matter?'

'It's OK.' She stopped in front of him, one hand raised to her face. 'I just have something in my eye.'

'Let me see.'

He set down his things as Penny stepped closer, and he brought her under the light, cupping her face as he tilted it to get a closer look. There was nothing obvious in either of Penny's eyes, and he had to resist the urge to step back from the cloying fragrance as her heavy perfume assaulted his senses.

'Oops, sorry. I didn't meant to interrupt.'

Kyle jerked away at the sound of Alexandra's voice, his hands dropping to his sides. He was furious at feeling he had been caught doing something he shouldn't. 'What is it?' he asked with more curtness than he intended, regretting the flicker of hurt surprise in Alexandra's smoky grey eyes, seeing her hand still raised in preparation to knock on the door.

'Nothing important. It can wait.' Her hand dropped, and her smile was coolly polite before she turned away. 'Have a good weekend, both of you.'

Then she was gone, and Kyle was left feeling more out of sorts and in the wrong than ever.

* * *

'I don't know why you employed her, Kyle. I've been very unimpressed. I hope it is only on a trial basis.'

Penny's words rang in Alex's ears as she beat a hasty retreat to the staffroom. At least she hadn't been close enough to hear Kyle's reply. The image of Kyle holding Penny, his head bent to hers, was now imprinted on her brain—along with the triumphant, calculated look in ice-blue eyes as the other woman had sent her a penetrating glare. So that was the lie of the land. Kyle and Penny. She hated the stupid disappointment that crushed her insides at the realisation. Fixing a bright smile on her face, she chatted with Lisa, Sheena and other staff members preparing to leave for the evening, and gathered up her own belongings, anxious to get home and in private lick the wounds she had no right to feel.

The last to leave, she turned to find the door blocked by Penny, the woman who was swiftly putting a damper on her time at Glenside. Alex's stomach clenched. In her early thirties, Penny had pale, milky skin with thick freckles across her cheeks which she tried to hide with an extra layer of already heavy make-up. Her ginger hair was worn scraped back from her angular face and restrained in a tight braid which fell down her back nearly to her waist. Tall and willowy, Penny was almost unnaturally thin, and was always immaculately turned out. Somehow Penny managed to make their nondescript nurses' uniform appear classy and, even with her thinness, figure-forming. On Alex's own lusher, more rounded body the clothes were loose, comfortable to work in but shapeless, and she often felt rumpled after a full day's work. So Penny's neat, petite perfection was galling. With eyes like shards of pale blue ice and a chilly personality to match, Penny was the coldest person Alex had ever met.

'I don't know what game you think you can play with Kyle,' Penny remarked, every word dripping with contempt as she ran her gaze over Alex and clearly found her lacking in every way. 'He is not available so I don't advise you making eyes at him. He may think to enjoy a little dalliance now and again, but he always comes back to me. Remember that. Although I very much doubt you could give Kyle anything he needs. He isn't into the homely, frumpy, unsophisticated type.'

Stunned at the attack, and decidedly miffed, Alex met Penny's cold, threatening blue gaze without flinching. Aside from the fact she hadn't been "making eyes" at Kyle, being described as homey, frumpy and unsophisticated rankled with her. Clearly, for whatever reason, Penny felt it necessary to stake her claim, and warn her off.

'I have no designs on Kyle Sinclair,' she informed her with a coolness she was far from feeling.

'See that you don't.' Again the condescending, malevolent gaze swept over her. 'Stay away from him…or I'll make your life here very difficult.'

Alex was anxious to succeed in this job, to fit in and to avoid any trouble or unpleasantness, so she held her tongue, feeling it wisest to save locking horns at this point. She banked down her own temper, unwavering under Penny's icy regard, only letting out a shaky breath when the other woman left without another word. No way would she allow Penny to browbeat her. But common sense told her that, whatever foolish notions nibbled at her, she should try very hard to avoid Kyle as much as possible and ignore her inappropriate attraction to him.

Kyle was clearly troubled and complicated, while she had enough changes and worries in her own life. She didn't need more. True, she did miss male company—going out, having fun, cuddling up with someone—and she was just about beginning to feel ready to step back into life in all respects. But, even if Kyle were not already involved, he was a bit too much of a man for her to handle and too disturbing for her peace of mind. And yet, even knowing all that, there were shadows in his eyes, ones she wanted to understand and erase. He seemed…lonely, keeping himself detached and removed, burying himself in work. It wasn't her business, but Alex felt instinctively drawn to him in a way she couldn't begin to explain. And, although he was out of bounds, otherwise attached to the unpleasant Penny, she ached for his unhappiness. However, the last thing she wanted was to cause trouble for him—and if anyone was trouble it was surely Penny Collins.

Better by far that she concentrate on her goals: re-establishing her career and saving her home. To do those two things she needed this job to be a success. And that meant putting enigmatic, sexy Kyle Sinclair right out of her mind.

CHAPTER THREE

ALEX sat in the car after her final scheduled Saturday house call, and took a few moments to stare at the scenery she loved so much and had missed while she had been living in England. She was about to put the car in gear and head home for a late lunch when her mobile phone rang, the display showing the incoming call was from the out-of-hours service. She answered without delay.

'Sorry to bother you, Alex. Are you nearing the end of your list?'

'I've just finished,' she replied, reaching for her notebook. 'Is there a problem?'

'I'm afraid so. I've had a call from the Campbells. They're regulars. In fact, Mr Campbell had a nurse visit yesterday but his wife has rung to say he is very uncomfortable. She was worried about bothering us but sounded upset, and I don't think it can wait until Monday,' her contact explained. 'Would you mind looking in on them?'

'Of course not. Can you fill me in on the basics? I don't have the notes and am not familiar with the patient.'

She was quiet for a few moments, taking down the details given to her about Mr Campbell's condition, his wife's call and the couple's address. Never mind lunch or salvaging something of the afternoon to tackle the thousand-and-one chores that awaited her. Her patients *always* came first.

'I'll go there now,' she promised once she had received the required information.

'Thank you, Alex.'

As she drove towards her new destination, Alex frowned as she reviewed the details she had been given about her additional patient, wondering what could have happened since a regular visit the previous day to cause him such discomfort. Twenty minutes later, she drew up outside a well-kept bungalow on the outskirts of one of the outlying villages well north of Rigtownbrae. Collecting her bag, she walked up the path to be met at the door by an anxious, harassed looking woman in her early sixties.

'Mrs Campbell?' Alex smiled to put her at ease and held out her hand. 'Hello, I'm Alexandra Patterson, the district nurse.'

'You're new here?'

'Yes. I just started this week. I'll be working part-time in the community and part-time at the surgery.'

A flash of relief lightened the concern in the woman's hazel eyes. 'Thank you so much for coming, I'm sorry to be such a bother.'

'Not at all, that's what we're here for. Shall we go in?'

'Of course.' Flustered, the woman stepped back to allow her inside the warm, neat home. 'Perhaps I should explain about my husband?'

Happy to take a few moments learning more of the history, Alex nodded in agreement. 'Please.'

'Bill has been ill for years with chronic obstructive pulmonary disease, and he's steadily deteriorating. His mobility is greatly reduced now, and he is increasingly breathless, on oxygen and various medications. He also has a catheter.' Mrs Campbell's hands knotted together in agitation. 'It was changed yesterday, but Bill's been so uncomfortable. It's not like him to complain, but I've been so worried, and I didn't want to leave him until Monday.'

Alex covered the restless hands with her own in reassurance. 'You did the right thing, Mrs Campbell, please don't worry.'

'Maria. And thank you.'

'No problem, Maria. Call me Alex.' With another smile, she picked up her bag. 'Perhaps I could just wash my hands and then I'll see your husband?'

'Yes. Yes, this way.'

Her hands washed and dried, Alex automatically squeezed a small amount of alcohol gel on her hands and carefully rubbed it in, smiling as Maria looked on.

'Not all the nurses use that. Or even wash their hands. Our regular nurse never does.'

Maria's admission had Alex's eyes widening in surprise. 'I see.' A flicker of concern rippled through her at the apparent lapse in basic hygiene.

'Sometimes Bill's well enough to sit up in his chair, but he didn't want to get out of bed today.'

Nodding at the explanation, Alex followed as Maria Campbell showed her through to a large, light room, and her gaze was drawn to the frail figure propped up in the bed. The oxygen was beside him, delivered through nasal cannulae, and one glimpse told her the man was in discomfort—his face pale, beads of perspiration on his forehead, a tremor in the hands that lay on top of the blankets.

'Bill, this is Alex, the new nurse.' Maria introduced them.

Weary brown eyes flickered open and focused slowly on her. 'Hello.'

'Pleased to meet you, Bill.' Alex moved closer to the bed and took one of the man's hands gently in hers, smiling at him.

'I'm sorry you're feeling so poorly. Let's see what we can do to make you more comfortable, all right?'

'Thank you, dear.' The voice wavered but conveyed his gratitude.

'I'll go and put the kettle on,' Maria offered, and Alex nodded her thanks, grateful to be allowed to attend to her patient alone.

After the door closed, she spent a few moments chatting to Bill, learning more about him and what was wrong before asking permission to begin an initial examination. She pulled on a pair of surgical gloves then drew back the bed linen and adjusted the man's clothes, struggling to hide her reaction when she discovered the state the poor man was in.

'The nurse yesterday left you like this?' she asked, her voice as even toned as possible.

'Yes.'

Alex sucked in a breath. 'I'm very sorry, Bill. I'll be as gentle as I can and have everything sorted out for you as soon as possible,' she promised, talking to the man to take his mind off her tasks, and her own mind off her anger and concern.

After sorting out the problems, she replaced Bill's catheter, making sure everything was correct this time and that he was comfortable, before checking his oxygen flow and familiarising herself with his medications and dosages. He was taking frusemide to reduce the oedema in his legs, a gentle oral laxative, oral prednisolone, plus bronchodilator drugs administered by nebuliser to aid his breathing. Doing a final check, she had one more nasty surprise, pausing as she spotted a pressure sore on the bony hip furthest away from her.

'This looks nasty, how long have you had it?' Alex asked, masking her worried frown as she walked round the other side of the bed and gently examined the angry, damaged flesh.

Bill took a moment to catch his breath. 'A short while.'

'Hasn't anyone done anything about it for you?' Shocked,

Alex held the man's hand again. 'Have you mentioned this to a nurse or doctor before?'

'I did, but I was told it was nothing to worry about.'

Nothing to worry about? Fuming inwardly, Alex kept her expression clear and her voice gentle. 'Who told you that—the nurse who visited you yesterday?' Alex wanted words with this person.

'Yes. She's my most regular nurse.' Bill paused and Alex waited, sensing he wanted to say more. 'I shouldn't talk out of turn, you being new and all, and she's a colleague of yours, too, but I don't like her. She's distant and always in a rush, and she can be quite rough. I often feel her mind isn't on the job. I wish I didn't have to have her visit so often.'

'Your comfort is the most important thing. You shouldn't be made to feel that way, Bill.' Concerned, she wondered how long this had been going on. 'Can you tell me her name?'

Again Bill hesitated, uncertain, and Alex was upset that the man felt unable to speak up for his needs. He clearly felt vulnerable, and perhaps was worried the nurse would somehow make things worse for him if he reported her. It was a sobering thought. His brown gaze slid to hers and anxiously away again. 'I don't want to put you in an awkward situation or cause trouble.'

'You're not. Honestly. You have a right to be treated with respect and dignity, and to receive the best possible care. But I understand if you feel uncomfortable. Just know you can tell me anything if and when you want too, all right?'

'Thank you.' A suspicion of moisture filmed the pensioner's brown eyes, and his grip was surprisingly strong as he held her hand.

Giving him what reassurance she could, Alex began to turn away when Bill murmured something. She moved back, her heart in her mouth. 'Sorry? I didn't hear you.'

'Nurse Collins,' he suddenly blurted, clearly anxious at imparting the information.

Penny had done this? Penny had neglected a patient, made him feel uncomfortable and afraid? Whilst Alex was loath to defend the other woman, she knew mistakes did occur and, however much she disliked Penny, she didn't want to believe that any nurse would deliberately mishandle a patient or treat one with such unconcern. And yet Bill was clearly worried and, from what he and Maria had said, this was not a one-off incident.

'I don't want you to worry about it, Bill. I'm going to put a dressing on your hip now to make things more comfortable, and I'll speak to one of the doctors on Monday morning,' she informed him, collecting what she needed from her bag. 'From now on, we will keep a proper eye on things and make sure that you are cared for. We can also investigate what is causing the pressure sore to develop and take steps to prevent it by trying to get you a better mattress for your bed, and a pressure-relieving cushion for your chair.'

'Thanks, dear, that would be kind.'

'You have a lovely view from here,' she commented as she worked.

The sick man's gaze turned out towards the Moffat hills in the distance. 'Aye. For years I used to walk up there, was even a volunteer for a time with the mountain-rescue unit. Nothing like the freedom and peace of those open spaces, not to mention all the history and folklore. Now I can't even walk across my own room.' He shook his head and gave her a sad smile.

Squeezing his hand again, Alex smiled back, sympathetic to how difficult and frustrating it was to come to terms with failing mobility after an active life—something she had been through with her father during his long illness. 'That should be more comfortable for you now, Bill. Is there anything else I can do for you while I'm here?'

'No. I'll be fine. You've been wonderful…and my wife is an angel. It's thanks to her I can stay at home.'

'Don't hesitate to let us know at once if there is anything you need,' Alex insisted, removing her gloves and adding them to the rubbish she had accumulated, before packing her things back in her bag. 'Never mind if it's the weekend or not.'

'Thank you, dear. I hope you'll be back to see me again.'

Alex took his hand one last time. 'I'm sure I will. I'll look forward to getting to know you, Bill.'

Leaving the man to rest, she threw the rubbish away then washed her hands again, before accepting the cup of coffee offered by Maria, drinking it in the small but neat kitchen while she filled her in on Bill's condition.

'I've been worried about that sore,' the woman admitted, her tiredness and concern evident.

'I've put a dressing on, and I've explained to your husband that I'll report it to the doctors and ensure Bill has proper care.'

Maria's hazel eyes lightened with relief. 'Thank you very much. You're so much easier to talk to than our usual nurse.'

'Don't ever be afraid to speak up for what you need, or complain if something isn't right. When the doctor comes to visit, you must feel free to explain what happened, to make your concerns known.' Alex was careful to keep her annoyance at Penny hidden. 'You and Bill are important and deserve our best efforts. If you don't feel satisfied, or there is anything you need, you can always ring the surgery.'

'I feel better about things now. I'm so grateful to you.'

Alex took her leave, a frown on her face as she returned to her car. She had only been at Glenside one week, and had already had a run-in with the unpleasant Penny. Whilst patient care was the number one priority, she felt uncomfortable and concerned about rushing straight in to accuse a colleague of poor working practice. She needed to check Bill Campbell's notes and see which doctor was responsible for him. Then she would make her report, and hope that both Bill and Maria would voice their worries and dissatisfaction with the nursing they had received. If not, and if things didn't improve rapidly, there was nothing for it but to face the wrath and report Penny herself. Alex would certainly be keeping a very close eye on the other nurse's methods from now on, and she hoped she would never find another patient who had been treated with the same lack of care.

Although she was keen to be finished, she took out her mobile phone and rang in to report that she had seen the Campbells. There was nothing else scheduled, and no other emergencies had been reported, so she was free to go home. Her call finished, Alex checked her watch. She was now much nearer Lochanrig than either Rigtownbrae or her own house, and she decided to take the opportunity to drop in on Nic and Hannah to collect a cat trap they had promised to lend her. Despite their busy schedules, the other couple were involved in caring for stray animals, an interest Alex shared with them. For the last few days she had been unsuccessfully trying to catch an unknown but injured feral cat she had seen hanging around her outbuildings at home—hence her need for the trap. Her decision made, she turned her car in the direction of Lochanrig.

'You trying to set some kind of record or something?'

Kyle turned with a frown at Conor's complaint, and watched his friend move up the path behind him, Nic bringing up the rear. 'Sorry?'

'You charged up here as if you had the hounds of hell on your tail.' Conor grimaced and shrugged out of his back pack, rummaging inside for a bottle of water. 'What's wrong with you?'

'Nothing.'

Nic joined them, his dark gaze watchful. 'You are meant to savour the journey, my friend. Do the hills not bring you enjoyment today?'

Smothering a sigh, Kyle eased off his own pack and sat down with his friends to eat their packed lunches. As he ate, he turned to stare at the view. They had walked up from the Devil's Beef Tub over Great Hill, Chalk Rig Edge and Whitehope Heights, undulating through hidden glens, along tumbling burns, past an old ruin and some cascades, before reaching the summit of Hart Fell over three hours after they had set out. The landscape was varied and magnificent, and the October day was warm, the sun low, the autumn colours showing off the region to its best effect. All part of the Southern Uplands, the Lowther and Moffat hills were as much a home to him as the Galloway hills were to Conor. One day he wanted to walk the whole Southern Upland Way, the two-hundred-and-twelve-mile path that ran from Portpatrick in the west to the North Sea cliffs at Cocksburnpath on the east coast. One day…

Kyle picked up his own bottle of water. Nic was right; this place usually brought him peace, which was why he had been so looking forward to their outing. But so far nothing had managed to banish the unease and inner disquiet that had gripped him for the last week or more. Tuning out Nic and Conor's banter, Kyle drew in a lungful of fresh air. With only his two best friends for company, he should have been relaxed, in his element, calm. But he was finding it harder than usual to slip into that zone today.

It was the first time they had all managed to get together for a day's hike like this since Conor had returned from honeymoon. Kyle had dreaded the late-summer wedding, having to stand up as Conor's best man—a reversal of roles from a few years before. But somehow he'd made it through, delivering a funny speech, being cheerful and chatty on the outside, while inside he had felt dead and filled with self-loathing because he was envious of his best friend's happiness. The pain of seeing Conor and Kate so much in love had seared inside him, the same way it did when he looked at Hannah and Nic together, the two of them still all over each other and blissfully happy.

How could he be jealous of his own friends, resentful that they had what he had lost? He hated himself for his selfish feelings. What kind of person had he become? These people had been there for him through everything these last eighteen months—understanding him, supporting him, picking him up when he'd been at the lowest, blackest point it seemed possible for a human being to sink. He loved them, would never have survived without them, and he would do anything for them... He *wanted* them to be happy. But it didn't ease the ever-present pain of loss and aloneness inside him.

'I know it wasn't easy for you, being my best man.' Conor spoke beside him, voice husky as he zeroed in with frightening perception on Kyle's train of thought. 'I want you to know how much it meant to me.'

'And to me. I was glad to do it, would have hated you asking anyone else. Kate's perfect for you, and I want you to be happy.'

Conor draped an arm across his shoulders. 'I know, buddy.'

'I'm sure you won't make the mess of things I did.'

'Kyle, it wasn't your fault,' Conor insisted, but the sincerity in his friend's voice failed to strip the inner guilt and sense of failure that plagued him.

'We're all worried about you,' Nic added. 'You are closing yourself off to everything but work, putting in all hours at the surgery, and doing more than your fair share with BASICS.'

Jaw set, Kyle stared unseeing at the landscape. 'Work is good for me. Work is all I need.'

'I understand loss, my friend.' Nic's accented voice was low, and Kyle nodded, knowing how the Italian had lost all his family and his fiancée in an earthquake some years before. Nic's experience had been terrible, leaving him alone, rootless, stricken. But his own loss was different—caused by betrayal, a complete abuse of trust, as well as grief. 'We all cope in our own way and go on at our own pace,' his friend continued, the lilting voice drawing him from his thoughts. 'I was a monk, denying my emotions and feelings and needs—until I met Hannah. Maybe it is time for you to begin to put the past behind and look to the future, no? To think about stepping back into life again.'

Unwanted, an image of Alexandra intruded into his mind. He frowned, struggling to push it away, remaining silent as he wrestled with his emotions, afraid of the chinks that were appearing in his carefully reinforced armour. Whatever Nic and Conor thought, he didn't want to feel anything again, to risk the hurt, to open himself to more pain. He had vowed he would never get involved with anyone else and he meant it—but something about Alexandra messed with his head. He had locked that side of himself away for a long time and he never planned on unlocking it. Instead he kept his feelings inside, closely guarded. Not like his friends. Nic was all Latin passion, wearing his heart on his sleeve, while Conor was the touchy-feely one, there for everybody, dispensing hugs as needed. Kyle didn't do touchy-feely. Not with just anyone. That all he had wanted this last week was to get touchy-feely with Alexandra—in private—was a shock to his system and a threat to his resolve. He didn't like it, he resented it, and he resented her for causing it.

They put their packs back on and prepared to continue their walk. Ahead of them lay the descent, some of it rough and steep, round Arthur's Seat, then down along Auchencat Burn and past Hartfell Spa, before curving through to Corehead and back to the Devil's Beef Tub and Annanhead Hill. As they set off, Kyle tried to set his confused thoughts aside, to clear his mind and enjoy the rest of the day.

'Hannah will never forgive me if I fail to find out all the news.'

'What news?' Kyle questioned, glancing at Nic walking beside him.

'About Alex, of course.' The Italian chuckled. 'How was her first week with you?'

Kyle smothered a groan. So much for not thinking about her. Clearly the wretched woman was going to continue to plague his existence, refusing to even allow him peace on his day off in the hills. 'She seems a competent nurse,' he allowed grudgingly, unable to keep the grumpiness from his voice.

'I hope she's settling in all right. It must be strange for her, getting back to work after all she's been through,' Nic commented.

'I wouldn't know. I've not spoken to her.' Kyle's frown deepened when he caught Nic and Conor exchanging an amused look, their eyebrows raised. 'What?'

Unconcerned at the glower he sent him, Conor smiled. 'You seem unusually flustered.'

'I'm not remotely flustered,' Kyle snapped. 'I thought we came up here to forget about work.'

'Sure!' Conor and Nic exchanged another smile.

His temper returning, Kyle marched on ahead, leaving his friends to trail in his wake, shutting his ears to their gentle teasing. If he found out that Hannah had, indeed, been playing some kind of game by trying to set him up with Alexandra he was going to be mad—madder still if Alexandra was in on the subterfuge. He just wished everyone, however well meaning, would leave him the hell alone.

* * *

'Alex! What a lovely surprise,' Hannah greeted.

Glancing over her shoulder at the car in the driveway, Alex hesitated. 'I should have rung first. If you have visitors…'

'Nonsense. It's just Kate. The guys have gone out walking in the hills for the day, so we're having a good chat.' Hannah smiled and gestured her inside. 'Come on in and join us.'

'Thanks.'

'You look very smart in your new uniform.'

Alex looked down at her rumpled tunic and grimaced, thinking what a contrast she was to the svelte, perfectly groomed Penny. Not that she wanted to think about *her* any more right now. 'I've just finished my Saturday shift, and as I was close by I thought I'd call in and collect that trap we talked about.'

'Of course. Still no luck catching the stray?'

'Not yet.'

Hannah, her long, auburn hair falling in fiery waves down her back, led the way into the cosy country kitchen where various animals vied for space in front of the range. Kate, GP wife of Conor Anderson, from the practice in Glentown-on-Firth some miles to the south-west on the Solway coast, sat at the table which held the remains of lunch. Alex eyed the remaining food and fought down the hungry rumble from her stomach.

'Hello, Alex.'

Meeting the attractive brunette's smile, Alex saw how blooming she was. Clearly married life with the irrepressible, sexy Conor was agreeing with her. 'Hi, Kate. Sorry to barge in.'

'It's good to see you again,' the other woman assured her with genuine pleasure.

Although she had only met Kate and Conor a couple of times here at Nic and Hannah's, Alex had taken to the couple immediately.

Hannah crossed to the range. 'Have you had any lunch,

Alex? Help yourself to anything. What would you like to drink—tea, coffee, hot chocolate, juice?'

'Thanks. Tea, if you're sure. I must admit I missed lunch, and those remaining sandwiches do look tempting! It seems for ever since breakfast.'

'Long shift?' Kate asked, sympathy in her dark brown eyes.

'More difficult than long.' Alex sat down and frowned. 'Especially at the end.'

A short while later they all had refreshments, and Alex was satisfying her hunger as they chatted about the animals and about Conor and Kate's honeymoon to Africa. The trip sounded so exciting and Alex sighed, wishing she could visit the Ngorongoro Crater in Tanzania one day, and see the wildlife in Kenya's reserves.

'I hear you have an elephant,' Alex commented, relaxed and replete after her meal, enjoying the company.

'Our favourite wedding present,' Kate agreed with a smile, as Hannah, balancing Wallace the ginger cat on her lap, reached out to take a photograph off the fridge door and passed it across.

Alex looked at the baby elephant enjoying a mud bath, and laughed. 'Oh, she's gorgeous!'

They chatted on for a while and then the talk turned to work. 'So, how was your first week?' Hannah asked, stroking the purring Wallace.

'Mixed,' Alex admitted truthfully. 'It's great getting back to nursing. I thought I'd be rusty, but after the first day nerves it was almost like I'd never been away. I've met some interesting patients and I like working both at the surgery and out in the community…'

'But…' Hannah prompted as the pause lengthened.

Alex took a sip of her second mug of tea. She didn't want to sound as if she was moaning, but it was nice to share her thoughts with understanding friends. 'The staff have been very welcoming. Mostly,' she added, seeing Hannah and Kate exchange a telling look.

'Don't tell me.' Hannah shook her head, a frown on her face. 'Poison Penny.'

'Is that what you call her?' Alex couldn't help laughing, some of her tension easing at the knowledge she wasn't alone in her dislike of the ice-cold nurse.

Kate's smile was wicked. 'Amongst other things! I've never met her, thankfully, but she's not one of Hannah's favourite people.'

'That's putting it mildly,' Hannah groused. 'So, you've had a run in with her already?'

'Let's just say Penny's made it quite clear she doesn't want me in Rightownbrae.'

Hannah's frown deepened. 'She's a bitch. I've never trusted her…professionally or personally.'

'Professionally?' Alex set her mug down and considered for a moment. 'Have you heard anything about her—as a nurse, I mean?'

'Nothing I have real evidence for. But we've had more than one patient join our list after leaving Glenside Surgery because they were either scared of her or complained about her lack of care,' Hannah confided after a moment.

'You look worried, Alex,' Kate murmured as a silence lengthened. 'Has something happened?'

Alex hesitated, wondering how to word her concern. 'I had an unscheduled call added to the end of my list today, that's why I'm so late. Penny had seen the patient yesterday, and he wasn't left in the best condition. I had to sort things out with his catheter and he confessed that he didn't like Penny, that she was sometimes rough and not very thorough, but he was anxious about complaining.' She paused a moment, remembering poor Bill's discomfort. 'I also found a pressure sore that had been neglected.'

'Oh, my.' Kate shook her head.

'I wish I could say I was surprised.' Hannah looked fierce, her gold-flecked green eyes filled with fiery sparks. 'What are you going to do?'

Sighing, Alex ran the fingers of one hand through her hair. 'First I'm going to check which doctor the patient is with and report the pressure sore. I've advised the patient and his wife to be frank with the doctor, and not be afraid to make a complaint or express how they feel about the care they have received—or lack thereof. I can't do anything yet, on one incident and hearsay. Penny is established at Glenside, I'm the incomer, and I need real evidence before accusing her officially. But you can bet I'll be watching her like a hawk and noting anything else suspicious. And if I find it... Well, regardless of her warnings to me and her being close to Kyle, I won't hesitate in putting patient welfare first,' she stated with raw determination, not wanting to consider what might happen if she did find something—or how Kyle might react to it.

A silence followed her statement and she looked at her two friends, wondering if they thought she was wrong or over reacting. Kate looked anxious, Hannah furious.

'What?' Alex asked after a moment, unable to stand the growing tension.

Kate shook her head. 'It's what you said about Kyle and Penny being close.'

'No way.' Hannah's voice rose. 'No way in hell is that woman getting her hooks into Kyle, not after all this.'

'Conor and Nic wouldn't let that happen,' Kate soothed, dark eyes expressing her worry.

Hannah seemed to relax at that, and nodded in agreement. 'That's true. We'll kidnap him if necessary. Penny's been subtly trying to insinuate herself into Kyle's life these past months, and he's been too distracted to notice.'

'Poor Alex looks startled!' Kate smiled.

'It's true I don't know all the ins and outs of the situation,' Alex allowed, thinking what an understatement that was given her utter confusion.

'Don't mind us; we just get protective of our own, especially Kyle.' Hannah's smile was affectionate and sad. 'He's had a horribly unhappy eighteen months.'

Kate looked down and rested a hand across her belly. 'Which is the reason I'm so worried at telling Kyle our news.'

'You're having a baby?' Alex smiled at the excitement in Kate's eyes and the flush on her face as her friend nodded. 'That's wonderful, congratulations!'

'Thanks! Conor and I are so excited.'

Hannah laughed. 'To say the least!' she teased.

'Mmm.' Kate sobered. 'It was hard enough telling you and Nic.'

'Oh, Kate, don't,' Hannah insisted sincerely, reaching for Kate's hand. 'I've known for a long time that I may never have children. Nic and I are fine with it. What happens, happens. And we haven't ruled out adoption or fostering. Until then, we have a whole menagerie of animals who need us, a big extended family of friends, not to mention the community around us and all our patients. Please don't worry about how we feel. We couldn't be happier for you. Honestly.'

Tears pricked Alex's eyes at the emotion-filled atmosphere.

Kate sucked in a breath and sent them a watery smile. 'Thanks. It doesn't make it any easier telling Kyle, though.'

'He'll be fine,' Hannah stated, but Alex could see the shadows in her eyes and wondered again what was going on, why there were undercurrents rippling around them.

'Why would Kyle mind?' she asked after another silence stretched between them.

Both women looked at her, and Hannah sighed. 'You don't know much about the story?'

'No.' Alex shrugged, trying to pretend she wasn't interested, but everything inside her was tying her in knots. 'I've heard a couple of comments about his marriage breaking up, that's all. Not that Kyle would tell me anything. He doesn't like me. I only got the job thanks to Robert and Elizabeth outvoting him.'

Again her friends looked at her in surprise. 'That's not like Kyle,' Kate pondered, sharing a glance with Hannah.

'Kyle's not been like Kyle for a while now.' Hannah set a wriggling Wallace back on the floor. The cat stretched with customary feline grace, before stalking across to the range to shift assorted cats and the three-legged Border terrier, Hoppity, aside so he could insinuate himself in the most comfortable spot. Sighing, sadness in her eyes and voice, Hannah continued. 'The divorce was difficult enough. Kyle's had a hard time trying to come to terms with that—but he's never recovered from, or properly grieved for, his dead baby.'

CHAPTER FOUR

ALEX forgot how to breathe. For a moment if felt as if her heart had stopped. Every part of her ached with pain for what Kyle had been through, the enormity of it only beginning to sink in. She registered Hannah's further explanations about a routine scan and the lack of movement, the absence of a heartbeat, of losing the baby late in the pregnancy as it died in the womb. From the first moment they had met she had sensed Kyle's dark unhappiness, his inner restlessness, his aloneness. She had heard that his marriage had ended. What she hadn't known, had never imagined, was the extent of his loss and how much hurt and torment he had been through.

As Hannah and Kate talked on, Alex was lost in her thoughts. What had happened to Kyle and his wife? How had losing their baby driven them apart rather than cemented them closer together? Why did Kyle feel so guilty? Had his wife, in her distress, blamed him—a doctor unable to save their child? She ached for his suffering. No matter that she hadn't known him long, no matter that she struggled to convince herself it was simply her nursing instinct—she could see how much Kyle was hurting and she hated it, wanted to help him despite his reserve and Penny's warnings.

But what could she do? Kyle had the very best of friends in Nic and Hannah, Conor and Kate. All four of them clearly cared for him and watched out for him. They were the ones closest to him, best placed and qualified to help him. And, whatever Hannah and Kate believed, there was the possibility, the likelihood, that Kyle had Penny too. On top of which, Kyle didn't even like her as she had discovered first hand this week with his reaction to her when they'd worked together or met in the surgery.

Male laughter followed by the sound of a door closing and coats being hung up in the hall announced the arrival of the men back from their hill walk, and Alex glanced at her watch, surprised how long she had lingered in the warm companionship with Hannah and Kate. She was even more surprised when it wasn't just Nic and Conor who came into the kitchen but Kyle, too. Dressed in black jeans and a thick black jumper, he looked delicious—sinfully attractive but darkly brooding. She could see the tension snap through him when he registered her presence, and the scowl on his face only confirmed her previous thoughts…as did his words.

'What are you doing here, Alexandra?'

'Kyle!' Hannah's reprimand was sharp and swift, filling the uncomfortable silence that followed Kyle's harsh demand.

'It's OK. I was just going, anyway. Lots to do at home.' Alex rose to her feet, maintaining as much dignity as she could. She said goodbye to Hannah, Kate, Nic and Conor, allowed herself a brief nod of acknowledgement in Kyle's direction, and turned to the door. 'Good to see you all again. And to hear your news,' she added with a smile at Kate. 'Thanks for the refreshments, Hannah.'

She was halfway home before she realised she had forgotten the cat trap, the very thing that she had gone to Lochanrig to collect. No way was she going back now.

* * *

'Thanks very much, Kyle. I hope you're pleased with yourself,' Hannah grumbled after Alexandra had left.

Hannah rose to her feet, kissed Nic, and then moved across to the range to put the kettle on. Kyle felt shame tighten his stomach, and he squatted down to make a fuss of a wriggling Hoppity, focusing on the dog because he couldn't bring himself to meet his friends' gazes, knowing he was in the wrong and that they were disappointed in him. Hell, he was disappointed in himself. But he'd been caught completely off-guard when he had walked into the kitchen and Alexandra had been sitting there, firing blood that didn't want to be fired, and stirring senses that didn't want to be stirred. Even in the shapeless uniform she'd looked amazing, all curvy and feminine, her grey eyes tempting and gentle. Eyes that had filled with hurt…thanks to him.

'You're not getting on with Alex?' Nic asked, puzzlement in his voice.

Cursing under his breath, Kyle rose to his feet and jammed his hands in the pockets of his jeans. 'I don't know her. She's a good nurse.'

'The best,' Hannah stated, clearly not ready to be mollified. 'Perhaps if you took the time to get to know her instead of being rude and unwelcoming you'd come to appreciate all her other qualities, too.'

'I don't socialise with staff.'

'That kind of uncharacteristic snobbishness is beneath you, Kyle. You used to socialise with everyone…and enjoy it. Now we hardly see you.' Kyle flushed under Hannah's admonishing gaze, knowing all his friends were shocked by his irregular behaviour, that, while they understood, the new distance he placed between himself and the rest of the world upset them. 'It must be a barrel of laughs working with you. Poor Alex.'

Conor shook his head, green eyes sad and confused. 'I

know you've had a rough time, but you never used to be so cold to people.'

'Alex has had a rough time, also,' Nic added, pouring tea into mugs as efficiently as he poured on the guilt. 'It is only a short time since she lost her father. They were very close. It's not been easy for her, and she's still grieving too.'

Which made him feel even worse, Kyle acknowledged, wishing they would change the subject and talk about something else. He didn't want to talk about Alexandra, didn't want to think about her. It wasn't that he didn't like her. He was scared he could like her far too much—that was the problem. She was a threat. He had promised himself there would be no room in his life ever again for a woman, and nothing had made him question that…until Alexandra. Experiencing an unwanted reaction to her had scared him, shocked him, and made him put up protective walls. He'd believed in dreams once. In love and happiness. But not any more. They weren't for him. His trust and his spirit had been broken. He had given everything he had to a woman but it hadn't been enough, and he had nothing left to give.

'Kyle?'

Kate's voice impinged on his consciousness and snapped him from his dark thoughts. 'Mmm?' He summoned a smile, watching as Conor sat down and drew Kate on to his lap.

'Conor and I have something to tell you…' She offered him a tremulous smile in return, exchanging glances with Hannah and Nic before cuddling further into her husband's arms.

'Is everything all right?' Kyle asked, concerned at the sudden tension in the room.

'Fine,' Conor reassured him, one palm resting over Kate's belly. 'We're pregnant.'

Kyle managed to hold it together, swallowing down a wave of pain as the familiar grief hit him. 'You are? That's great!

Congratulations!' Crossing the room, he gave Kate a kiss and clasped Conor's shoulder.

'We're conscious what it means to you. There was never going to be a right time to mention it.' Kate took his hand in hers, her gaze reflecting the way her anxiety for him tamed her inner joy. 'We don't want to add to your hurt.'

'You're not, don't be daft. I'm delighted for you,' Kyle insisted, plastering a smile on his face, genuinely happy for his friends despite his own emptiness and bitter sense of loss.

Tears glistened in Kate's dark eyes, and Kyle felt choked as she drew his hand to her lips and kissed him. 'Thank you. Conor and I want all three of you to be godparents.'

'We should have a meal out or get together to celebrate,' Kyle suggested with forced brightness, both touched and horrified at the thought of being so closely involved in the baby's life, wanting it, but dreading it too.

'A good idea, my friend.' Nic smiled, and Kyle sensed the Italian fully understood the mixed emotions rampaging inside him. 'We'll arrange something, no, next time we are all off duty at the same time?'

Everyone agreed. They talked on for a while, and Kyle was thankful when the time came when he could reasonably make his excuses to leave for home. He needed some space to think, to get himself back together.

'Are you going straight back to Rigtownbrae?' Hannah asked.

'I am.'

'Could you do me a favour?'

'Sure,' he agreed, anxious to make amends for his earlier bad mood.

Hannah nodded, a suspicious gleam in her gold-flecked green eyes. 'Good. As Alex was chased off in such a rush she didn't take the cat trap she came here for, and she'll be wanting to catch the injured feral she has hanging around her place as soon as possible. You can go down the back road and drop it off on your way. I'll give you directions.'

'Of course.' Seeing the amusement in Conor's eyes, knowing he had been suckered, Kyle hid his reluctance and took the piece of paper Hannah gave him. It really wasn't out of his way and was the least he could do, given his boorish behaviour.

The back route to Rigtownbrae from Lochanrig was wonderfully quiet and scenic in the time before dusk, sparsely populated with farms and country cottages, the wide glen with a mix of rolling farmland and pockets of woodland marked on one side by the lazy curve of a small river, and the other protected by the gentle arc of hills. Despite the darkness of his raging thoughts, the tranquility of the setting brought a measure of calmness. Having grown up on his parents' farm in Ayrshire, he longed for the countryside, still missed the rural house and small patch of land that had been home while he'd been married, but which had been sold in the division of property at the time of the divorce.

He was surprised when he arrived at the address Hannah had given him. He'd had no idea that Alexandra lived on a small, isolated working farm. There were no other properties within sight, and the single-storey sprawling cottage, whitewashed under a slate roof, sat back from the road in a picturesque spot and had a range of outbuildings, including two large barns, laid out around a small yard behind the house. A wave of longing swept through him and he shook his head. It was perfect, exactly the kind of place he would love to live, so much more peaceful and homely and welcoming than the bleak little house he now occupied in town. He wondered what help Alexandra had, how much work she had to do herself here since her father's illness and death, and how she managed it all with a full-time job. It made him realise how little he knew about her, how successful he had been in blanking out any details of her real existence, because at a subconscious level he had known from the first second he had seen her that she was a threat to his resolve, his aloneness.

Part of him wanted to turn and run, forget his promise to Hannah about delivering the cat trap, because that sense of threat was very real just sitting here, imagining seeing Alexandra on her home turf. Angry with himself, he left the car, collected the trap from the back and carried the unwieldy contraption towards the house. There were two doors on the one long side of the building. One was clearly a more formal front door, but further along was a back door off the kitchen where a few half-wild cats scattered from their positions near the porch at his approach, diving for cover under bushes or around the side of the house. Down a path between two outbuildings, he could see an open area where several chickens, watched over by an impressive, strutting cockerel, pecked and scratched contentedly on the ground. He would love to linger, to explore, to learn more about this place, but he didn't dare.

Drawing in a deep breath, he rang the bell at the front door, hearing a dog barking inside and, when it stopped for a few moments, the faintest sound of running water. He rang again but still no one answered. Alexandra's car was in the drive, so she was clearly home—either out in the buildings or surrounding fields somewhere, or inside…taking a shower. The last thought was enough to stir his mind with uncomfortable images and tighten his insides. He'd done what Hannah had asked. Delivered the trap. She hadn't said he had to hang around indefinitely to hand it to Alexandra in person. Taking the coward's way out, cursing himself as all kinds of fool, he walked to the other entrance, opened the outer porch door, set the trap down, and scribbled a brief note on the back of the piece of paper Hannah had given him. That would have to suffice. He'd done his bit. With far too many confused and dangerous thoughts plaguing him, it was better by far that he leave now while the going was good and without having to endure another face to face encounter with the woman who had managed to thoroughly unsettle his carefully guarded and reconstructed world.

'Success!'

Sunday morning had dawned cool, crisp and autumnal, the low sun slanting its way over the line of the hills. Alexandra's first task after dragging herself out of bed at far too early an hour had been to pull on her clothes and tiptoe to the barn to see if the injured cat had succumbed to hunger and taken itself inside the cat trap. It had! Fabulous. Careful not to cause the wounded stray too much stress, she approached the hissing, spitting, decidedly miffed animal and covered the trap with a blanket. All she had to do now was phone the vet and arrange to drop the animal in so it could be sedated and examined. If its injuries were treatable, she would bring the cat home when it was well enough and let it find its place amongst the assorted felines already populating her property.

Back in the house after feeding the stock, letting out the chickens and completing a few of the dozens of other chores that needed doing, she made herself a quick breakfast and a much-needed first cup of coffee. Aside from a trip to the vet, she hoped to spend the day catching up on the growing list of jobs that were escaping her and with which she was falling ever further behind since she had begun nursing again full time. Thankfully, Jim Buchan, a retired stockman who had worked most of his life on a nearby farm, liked to keep his hand in, and had been helping her father and now her around the place for years. He had a dicey heart and had been pensioned off, much to his disgust, but he enjoyed his place with the Pattersons and Alex made sure he was careful not to overdo things. He was an absolute godsend, and she knew she would never keep the place ticking over without him.

Sipping her coffee, she sighed, finally admitting that all her frantic thoughts were to keep her mind away from the one thing that had disturbed her unduly since yesterday. Kyle had been at her home. She'd been in the shower when the bell had rung, and by the time she had ventured out and made herself decent her caller had gone. But she had found the trap and the note, and a ridiculous fluttering had started in her stomach at the realisation that—albeit under instruction from Hannah—Kyle had dropped the trap by for her, had been just outside, a few feet away, while she had been naked under the hot spray of water. Heat crossed her cheeks and she told herself what an utter idiot she was being. She was just thankful she had avoided another difficult encounter with him, that he had left the trap and gone when she had taken so long to answer the door.

The phone rang, putting an end to her unsettling musings, and she set down her mug and reached out for the receiver. 'Alex Patterson.'

'I'm sorry to do this to you, especially after yesterday and it being your first week, but we've had a nurse phone in sick. Could you possibly cover some of the essential calls?'

Alex stifled a groan, seeing another day slipping away from her but knowing she couldn't, wouldn't, say no. 'I have to go to Rigtownbrae anyway, so tell me what's on the list.' Tiredness laced her voice.

'You're a star,' the woman thanked her sincerely. 'I hate asking you to do this, but we're desperate.'

'It's all right.'

After writing down the list of calls, addresses and subsidiary information she needed, Alex terminated the call and placed two more, one to old Jim asking if he minded coming in to mind the animals after all, and one to the vet, Alistair

Brown, husband of Shona who was a district nurse at Lochanrig, to arrange with him about dropping off the injured cat. That done, she set off to change back into the uniform she had hoped to neglect for at least one day.

Having seen to the cat and the handful of calls that had needed her attention, Alex stopped off at the surgery. With a hectic day ahead on Monday, she planned to write her report on the Campbells now while she had the opportunity to look over the notes, and also write up the details of the calls she had completed that morning. All was quiet as she let herself into Glenside and, after making herself a cup of coffee to accompany the sandwich she had brought with her, she collected the notes she needed and went through to the nurses' room where she made a start sorting through them and writing up her calls.

She left the Campbells until last. Glancing at Bill's notes, she groaned. She'd had a one in three chance which doctor would turn out to be his GP. It was lucky she wasn't a betting woman or she'd be seriously out of pocket with her bad run of luck. Needless to say, the name on the notes was Kyle's. Which made the issue of Penny's neglect all the more challenging and complicated to deal with. Hell. She ran her fingers through her hair, lost in thought.

'What are you doing here? I thought Penny was on duty today and you were supposed to be having time off.'

A hand pressed over her heart, Alex swung round on her chair in shock at the sound of Kyle's deep, husky voice. 'You scared me. I didn't hear you come in.' He stared at her, an enigmatic expression in his midnight blue eyes, and she struggled to get her breathing back under control and find her voice. 'The service called me in to work this morning as someone rang in sick.' She hadn't known that it was Penny, but she wouldn't put it past the woman to have done it on purpose. Was that why Kyle had come to the surgery, hoping to see Penny? Confused and annoyed, she managed a shrug. 'I had to come to town to the vet so I thought, as tomorrow is looking so hectic, I would take the chance to write up the notes now.'

'Right.' He continued to stand and stare at her, making her heart thud and her skin prickle. Did every woman Kyle looked at turn to a boneless puddle in front of him? Was it just her? Her brain congealed, her thoughts fragmented, every atom of her femininity flared with heat under the intensity of that searing blue gaze, but she couldn't force herself to look away from him. 'You caught the cat, then?'

'Um, yes. Thank you for dropping off the trap,' she managed, feeling as flustered as a nervy, besotted teenager.

Kyle eased his hands into the pockets of his skin-tight jeans, drawing her attention to the perfection of his athletic, muscular frame encased in the faded blue denim that hugged his body like a second skin, topped with a rough Aran sweater, the cream colour accentuating his maleness and his rakish good looks.

'Is the cat badly hurt?' he asked now, and Alex felt as if her brain was on go-slow as she struggled to process the simple question.

'I'm not sure yet.' She swallowed, pausing to lick suddenly dry lips, alarmed when Kyle's sultry gaze followed the movement of her tongue. Hell! She spun away and tried to focus back on the notes in front of her. 'Um, Alistair Brown is taking care of it.'

'Good. He's an excellent vet.'

'Yes.'

Alex squeezed her eyes closed and prayed Kyle would go away. This was excruciating. Her heated awareness of him was painful and becoming embarrassing.

'I'll let you get on, then,' he murmured after another agonising moment.

'Right. Thank you.'

He still showed no sign of leaving, however. 'I'm sorry you've had to come in today; you've worked hard this week.'

'I don't mind.'

'Still, it must be difficult with your farm needing your attention, too.' She glanced at him, surprised at the interest in his tone. 'It's an impressive place.'

'I like it.' Which was an understatement.

Frowning, Kyle pulled his hands free of his pockets and folded his arms across his broad chest. 'It's been hard for you. I'm very sorry about your father.'

'Thanks.'

Uncharacteristic tears stung her eyes, not just at the grief of losing the man she had loved so much, and who had been as much friend as father all her life, but at the unexpected softening of Kyle's manner towards her, the empathy and sincerity of his voice. What he said was true—it had been hard holding things together, keeping them going now. Money was tight. She'd not had any proper earnings for over a year, since she had first come home to care for her father. And it wasn't as if the farm made any money. It barely ticked over, was certainly nothing like it had been in her childhood when her father had been well and fit and keen. She had been shocked at how run down things were when she had come home, and it had sunk in hard just how much her father had been struggling until then. Fortunately there were no debts, so they had just about kept their heads above water. She would never make any money out of the farm but she was determined to keep it on partly, she had to admit, for sentimental reasons. Much of the land was rented out to neighbouring farmers now, but she couldn't bring herself to give up completely, and certainly she could never move away. She kept her hand in with some stock, thanks to Jim Buchan's help, but it was just a hobby now for her and Jim. It was the job here at Glenside which was providing her with the only way she could survive and stay in the home she loved.

'It's not easy, but I'm coping,' she answered, realising Kyle was waiting for her reply.

Worry creased his forehead. 'You have some help?'

'Yes. I'm fine.' If she said it often enough, she might just believe it.

'OK.' Kyle straightened and moved backwards into the corridor. 'I'll be in my room, I've got paperwork to do. Let me know if you need anything.'

Alex managed a smile. 'I will.'

As she heard his footsteps retreat through the building, she leaned on her desk, trying to bring her frantic pulse back under control and draw air into starved lungs. The man was dangerous under normal circumstances—being nice, he was positively lethal.

Determined to concentrate on what she was doing and put all thoughts of Kyle out of her mind, she phoned the Campbells to check on Bill, relieved to find he was comfortable, then returned her attention to her report of her visit to him the day before. Which meant thoughts of Kyle intruded once more. She was going to have to tell him what had happened and explain the pressure sore to him. Frowning with concern, she nibbled her bottom lip as she began to carefully word her assessment.

How was he supposed to get any work done, knowing Alexandra was mere yards away? His concentration was shot to pieces. Kyle slumped on to his chair, not wanting to admit either how good it had been having a normal conversation with her or the way his body reacted just being in her presence.

Thoughts of yesterday had kept him awake most of the night, especially the news from Conor and Kate about their baby. He'd been out for a punishing run, then was called to a multiple car pile-up on the motorway which had kept him busy for much of the morning in his capacity as BASICS doctor on call. The house had felt claustrophobic when he'd returned, so he'd walked up to the surgery to tackle the mountain of paperwork on his desk. Anything to try and forget, to not brood. Not that it was helping. Especially after finding Alexandra there.

He'd arranged for a huge bouquet of flowers to be delivered to Conor and Kate in Glentown-on-Firth, expressing his genuine delight for them, and despite his own loss he knew he would spoil their baby rotten and be a devoted godfather. But deep inside it still hurt. He pressed a hand to his chest, trying to ease the stabbing ache that seldom left him, the huge hole of emptiness that had swallowed him these last eighteen months.

Sighing, knowing he was torturing himself but unable to stop, he took out the now rumpled photograph he carried with him always, the only one he had, taken from the last scan when his baby had still been alive. A time when life had been good and the future had held promise. A time before his whole world had fallen apart. Dragging the fingers of one hand through his hair, he leaned back in his chair and frowned, the pain tightening inside him as he recalled the moment it had become apparent that something was terribly wrong. The moment when he and Helen had been unable to speak to each other any more. Why hadn't the shared tragedy of losing their baby pulled them together instead of driven them apart?

He had known Helen for as long as he could remember. They had grown up in a small rural community in Ayrshire, he on the family farm, she the daughter of the local postmaster. She had always been delicate, shy, ethereal, and he had protected her from school bullies and teenage hurts, caring for her, watching out for her, at first like a big brother. They had been good friends for years before anything deeper had happened, at least on his side. He'd dated a few other people in the years he'd been away at medical school, which was where he had met and befriended Conor Anderson. But Helen had always been there, waiting faithfully and patiently for him, never seeming to want anyone else. He swallowed down a humph of bitter, humourless laughter at that thought.

After qualifying, he'd secured his post in Rigtownbrae, and once he'd been settled and in a position to offer Helen something he had asked her to marry him, as had always been expected by both their families and themselves. Was that why they had done it—expectation? Familiarity? Comfort? Yes, he'd liked her, cared about her—but had he loved her as he should or had it been more affection, like a sister or best friend? Helen had claimed she trusted him, loved him, wanted to be with him. Yet marriage had never really suited her, not the most intimate part of it anyway.

Helen had been so shy, so scared of passion, of sex, so he'd always kept things gentle so as not to alarm her, locking away any possibility of a more fiery need within him. Although they might not have lusted after each other, life had been good. They'd been happy. They'd had friendship, trust and respect. Or so he'd thought. But the marriage had become increasingly shaky. Would the baby have cemented things? Probably not. Although he'd longed for a family. He and Helen had talked about everything…until the day the wheels had come off and thrown everything into a chaotic, hurtful, embittered mess. Then he had found out he didn't know Helen at all. He had lost her as well as his child. And along the way he had lost himself too. He wasn't sure he'd ever find himself again or if there was anything left to find.

He had been emotionally crippled by the grief, the betrayal, the loss. He'd forced himself to face a stark realisation. He knew with the benefit of hindsight that he had never loved Helen in the fullest sense of the word, had never felt those hundred and one things he should have felt when truly, deeply, helplessly in love—like needing her very presence to breathe, aching to hear her laugh, wanting to share every tiny joy, triumph and pain with her. He had loved her—had just not been *in love* with her. But he had genuinely cared for her, had given her everything he had to give of himself, devoted himself to her and all she had wanted. Helen had needed him and that had been enough. Once. Sort of. Or so he had thought. Until she had thrown it all back in his face. He had spent so long denying himself that now he didn't know who he was any more.

He had buried his grief for his lost child because Helen had gone to pieces and he'd needed to keep it together to help her through her depression. And he'd still had to be there for his patients. He'd been giving to everyone and feeling that no one had really understood him. His friends had helped, especially Conor, but they had their own lives, problems and joys, and he'd not felt able to explain the extent of his inner torment. He'd gone off the rails for a few weeks. Never the type to lose himself in a bottle or chase after a load of women, he had drowned his pain by taking far too many stupid risks out climbing and mountain biking, not caring if he hurt himself—or if he ever came back. Conor and Nic had saved his rear more than once and had talked some sense into him, hauling him back on track again. And Conor was a patient and understanding listener. Kyle had talked—a lot—just never quite getting to the core of the pain inside him, never really letting go and grieving properly.

Penny, new to the practice, had been sympathetic, full of advice, taking it upon herself to befriend both him and Helen, spending time with each of them. But things had worsened, not improved, the gaping chasm between him and Helen continuing to widen instead of close. He'd thrown himself into work while Helen had turned to Colin, an old childhood friend of theirs from school—and, unbeknown to him, Helen's former boyfriend while he'd been away at medical school. The man she said she wished she had married in the first place.

Kyle closed his eyes on the memories, the pain, his body rigid with tension, a nerve pulsing along his jaw. Setting down the photograph, he scrubbed his hands over his face, wishing he could wipe out everything that had happened, make it all go away.

Alex stood at the door to Kyle's room and bit her lip, uncertain about disturbing him. He had his eyes closed and was clearly tired, a dark shadow of stubble outlining the strength of his jaw and adding to his masculine good looks. She hated to bother him, but she really did need to tell him about Bill Campbell. Sucking air into her lungs, trying to ignore the way her pulse sped up just at the sight of him, she tapped on the door.

He looked up, dark lashes lifting slowly, and the pain revealed in his tortured eyes took her breath away.

CHAPTER FIVE

'KYLE, what's wrong?'

'Nothing.' He shook his head, whether trying to convince her or himself she didn't know. 'What did you want, Alexandra?'

She hesitated a moment, aching for him, wanting to help but scared of overstepping his boundaries. He was so controlled, so guarded...yet clearly enduring so much inner torment. Had he heard about Conor and Kate's baby? Had that news put the sadness on his face? Deciding to play things cool for now, she outlined the issues regarding her visit to Bill Campbell yesterday, seeing Kyle frown, his concern increasing as she explained about the problems and about finding the pressure sore.

'Why on earth has no one reported this before?' he demanded, dragging his fingers through his hair in agitation.

'I don't know.' She paused, unwilling to launch straight into a verbal attack on Penny, especially when she didn't yet know the full extent of the relationship between the nurse and Kyle. 'I'd never been to the Campbells before, so I'm not familiar with the case.'

'No. No, of course you aren't. Thank you for filling in and for being so thorough.'

'It's my job.'

Midnight blue eyes watched her and she swallowed, feeling new heat wash through her under the intensity of his regard. 'One that clearly means a lot to you and which you are very good at.'

'Thank you.' His approval made her warm inside.

'I'll make sure I pay the Campbells a visit in the next couple of days and check on Bill myself,' he promised, making a note in his diary.

Again Alex hesitated. 'I think they are nervous about expressing their views.'

'You mean they are wary of complaining about things they are unhappy with concerning Bill's care? They're afraid of some backlash?' he demanded, his expression darkening.

'Possibly. Yes.' She shifted uncomfortably under his enigmatic gaze. 'It's not uncommon.'

'Sadly, that's true. But they deserve the best of care, and it's our job to see that they get it. Thank you for the warning, I'll be sure to draw them out if I can. If necessary we'll adjust the nursing schedule. I won't have patients frightened to speak up if something is wrong.'

Satisfied with his sincerity, and that she had done her best to alert Kyle to the situation without attacking Penny outright, Alex nodded. 'I've written it up if you'd care to look over the notes before you go to see them.'

Stepping forward to put the packet on his desk, she looked down, her attention caught by the small black-and-white photograph that lay in front of him. Her throat tightened with emotion as she recognised what it was and a wave of compassion rolled through her. That Kyle was aware became apparent when he all but snatched the notes out of her hand and set them down on top of the baby scan photograph, his hands clenching to fists on top of the pile.

Unthinking, knowing only a desperate need to comfort him, she stepped round the desk and closed the gap between them. 'Kyle…' she murmured, resting a hand on his shoulder, feeling him tense beneath her touch.

'Forget it.' His voice was raspy, unfamiliar, and his head was bent as he refused to meet her gaze.

'You spoke with Kate and Conor yesterday,' she pressed gently, aware of the way his body became even more rigid under her hand. 'You know about their baby?'

'Yes.'

She bit her lip, stepping warily. 'Would you like to talk about it?'

'What for?'

'Sometimes it helps to share things rather than keeping it all inside,' she ventured, unperturbed by the roughness of his voice, and all too aware of the firm flesh and play of muscle her fingers detected through his jumper.

'Alexandra…'

She could tell that he didn't find it easy to express his feelings, and guessed he hadn't allowed himself to grieve for his lost child or to acknowledge how much it continued to hurt him. Not to other people, at least. Of their own volition, her fingers moved, her hand rubbing across his back, soothing his tension.

'I expect you feel both happy and sad at the same time.' She took the risk, hoping to draw him out, relieved that he had not immediately rejected her touch, her presence. 'That's understandable. But you feel angry with yourself.'

'Disgusted,' he bit out, surprising her, both that he had spoken at all and at the depth of emotion in that one word.

'But—'

'They're my best friends, I'm thrilled for them.' His hands flexed on the desk then clenched into tight fists again. 'But I feel awful for resenting them, too, for reacting like this.'

He sounded so lost and alone. Biting back a fresh surge of emotion, she kept her voice calm. 'That's normal, Kyle. Human. It's not wrong, and it doesn't mean you aren't happy for them or that you're a bad person. They understand. Truly. They know how much you care, but they also know you are still grieving for your own loss.'

He swore under his breath, and for a second she was scared she had gone too far. 'I haven't grieved. I can't grieve. I'm still too angry, too lost, and feel so guilty.' The admission was torn from him, shocking them both.

'What happened?' she ventured, anxious to encourage him to ease some of the hurt, to let it out.

She didn't think he was going to speak. The electric silence dragged on. He didn't look at her, but nor did he move away from the touch of her hand, so she stood her ground and waited. Everything inside her tightened when he finally started to speak, telling her almost clinically about the loss of his child and the way things had fallen apart afterwards.

'Nothing I did was right. Within a very short time Helen found solace with someone else. She left me for Colin, brazenly setting up home with him, going for the quick divorce, unashamed at admitting the adultery,' he explained, an odd mix of detached coldness and hot despair lacing his tone. 'They married as soon as the divorce was through, and Helen was pregnant again straight away. Now, eighteen months on from the moment our world collapsed and our baby died, she and Colin are happier than ever and have healthy twin boys.'

'Oh, Kyle,' she murmured, shocked by his story, aching for his loss, the sense of betrayal, rejection and confusion he hadn't been able to hide.

'It still hurts. Helen didn't care about me, didn't love me, didn't want a child with me. She was even relieved to have lost our baby, because it bought her freedom from our marriage.' Alex gasped at the callousness of it, the bitter anguish evident in every word he spoke. How could anyone have treated him that way, brought him so much added pain? 'Hell, I was such a fool. I tried, I really tried to make it work, to give her everything, but it wasn't enough. The Helen I thought I knew was sweet and innocent and shy—turns out I never really knew her at all.'

Alex was still trying to absorb everything he had told her when he suddenly moved, shocking her as he drew her closer and wrapped his arms tightly around her, one round her waist and one round her hips. Her pounding heart melted and she acted instinctively, cradling his head against her abdomen, one hand holding him close as she tried to absorb his pain, the other stroking the silken strands of his dark hair. She was scarcely able to breathe with the urgency and desperation of his embrace. Tears stung her eyes but she fought them back, knowing he wouldn't want them. She closed her eyes against them, every part of her aware of his closeness, the feel of him, his warmth, the woodsy, earthy scent of him, his hardness against her soft curves.

In silence she held him, knowing he just needed to be close to someone, anyone, trying to give him her strength and comfort. Her fingers sank into the lustrous thickness of his dark hair, to massage and soothe. She heard him murmur something but couldn't catch what it was, then his hands were tightening on her before slowly moving over her back, and she sucked in a shaky breath as the sexual tension ratcheted up and desire took over from platonic solace. Need flared inside her, inappropriate, shocking in its intensity, as his face turned more into her, nuzzling against her stomach, the top of his head brushing against the undersides of her breasts. Her whole being felt on fire in response, her fingers trailing over the warm skin at the back of his neck.

Between one heartbeat and the next, Kyle released her with stunning abruptness and all but pushed her away from him, leaving her staring in shock and confusion, her legs feeling shaky and unable to hold her upright. What had just happened?

Kyle shook his head, trying to clear it. He had to be insane. Alexandra had offered comfort and understanding to a colleague, but all he had suddenly been able to think about was the overwhelming urge to sweep everything off his desk, lay her down on it and satisfy the urgent desire raging through him. He hadn't had feelings like that in a long, long time. Hadn't wanted to. And no one had interested him in the slightest. Until Alexandra. Feeling her soft, lush curves against him just now, breathing in the intoxicating fragrance of her—like a wildflower meadow on a warm summer day, fresh and natural—had stripped away all his common sense and decency.

What the hell was he thinking? How much had he revealed, uncharacteristically spilling his guts to her like that? Dismay and shame surged through him. He couldn't look at her. He just wanted to forget what had happened, what he had told her, how she had felt in his arms… How he had felt holding her so tightly.

'Kyle…'

He couldn't deal with all the ramifications of her caring, of her even being here close to him. 'You should go,' he rasped more harshly than he'd intended.

'You know where I am if you ever want to talk. In confidence. If you decide not to, I understand that too.'

Her voice sounded husky, shaky, full of compassion, and he couldn't stand it.

'Just go, Alexandra. Please.'

Tackling Penny was not going well. Kyle sighed and ran the fingers of one hand through his hair. He'd been concerned by what Alexandra had told him following her visit to the Campbells, even more so after he had been to talk with the couple himself, examined Bill, and then coaxed them into confiding in him about their problems with Penny's care. He looked at the redhead now, sitting across the other side of the desk from him, pale blue eyes cold as ice, her mouth drawn in a tight line of annoyance and affront that he had questioned her. Quite why he had kept Alexandra's name out of things he couldn't say, only that he had felt the vibes between the two women. He was already fed up with Penny dropping hints and snide remarks about Alexandra's credentials as a nurse at every available opportunity, implying she was slow, inefficient, not worth her place on the team. Her efficiency was one thing he had no doubts about. Everything else left him completely befuddled.

'All I was asking, Penny, was why the pressure sore went untreated and unreported.' He held on to his patience with difficulty.

'I've been here a long time, and you cast judgement on my skills now?'

'I'm not casting judgement.' He drew in a steadying breath, tired of the argument. 'I have to ask, having seen the situation for myself. I know how hectic the job can be, that things can slip past us. My only concern is for the well-being of our patients, you know that. Please understand. None of us here want to compromise on patient care.'

Penny rose to her feet, her body tense. 'I don't need to be told how to do my job.'

Kyle couldn't excuse her attitude, but having had no complaints about her before he decided to let things go—for now. She was miffed, but hopefully some of the friendly advice would sink in. Maybe he had been too wrapped up in his own troubles these last months. From now on he would be taking much closer notice of what went on around him, and he would be talking with his partners, Robert and Elizabeth, about monitoring the care their patients received from all the practice staff.

'You've changed, you know.' Penny crossed her arms and glared at him, her expression hard. 'Since *she* came.'

'She?'

'Alex Patterson.'

Penny all but spat the name at him, and his own tension increased. 'Alexandra has nothing to do with this.' His gaze narrowed as he watched Penny, unable to understand her antipathy. Whenever he had seen Alexandra with patients he had been nothing but impressed, and no one but Penny had a bad word to say about her.

'You'll make a fool of yourself over her, Kyle.'

'I don't know what you're talking about.'

Penny gave a snort of derision. 'I've seen how you look at her. I agree it's past time you got on with living again, but not with her. Alex is a player, Kyle. She has some poor sap of a fiancé on hold, waiting for her back in England. Did you know that? And she's dating someone here. I've seen her out with Drew Grainger. She's playing games with you, and is not to be trusted. I just don't want you to get hurt again,' she finished, sounding sincere, but with a calculating expression in her eyes that made him suspicious.

After Penny flounced from his room, Kyle leaned back in his chair and frowned, lost once more in dark thoughts. He didn't want to listen to Penny, didn't want to doubt, found it hard to believe that Alexandra was anything but genuine. But then he had never imagined that shy, sweet Helen was playing him for a fool, either, and look how wrong he had been about her.

He was confused and unsettled. He didn't want to feel like this, had vowed he would never get involved with anyone else again, but since the moment of meeting Alexandra he had felt tempted, tested, uncertain, and was fighting an attraction he didn't want to feel. Were his instincts about Alexandra really so far out? Did she really have a fiancé waiting in the wings down south? Was this just a temporary job before she went back to her old life with him? And was Penny right about Alexandra seeing Drew? He'd always got on well with the local firefighter on a professional and casual level, but the man was reputed to be popular with the ladies. Had Alexandra fallen for that charm? After everything that had happened with Helen, he couldn't go through all that again. He found it so hard to trust. Something about Alexandra drew him, messed with insides, but he couldn't risk himself—not again.

The next weeks settled into a pattern and passed quickly with shifts at the surgery and out in the community, all the usual work combining with unexpected minor emergencies and the ongoing programme of annual influenza vaccinations. Throughout the hectic time Alex loved her job, adored her patients and came to know and appreciate her colleagues, the team of nurses she worked with both at the surgery and out in the community, all supportive and friendly. Except for one. She avoided Penny as much as possible but, when they did happen to run into each other at Glenside, she closed her eyes to the other woman's icy glares, and her ears to the short, sharp barbs Penny flung her way.

She had no idea what Kyle had done about the Campbells, or if he had spoken to Penny, but she had noted with relief that, on the days Bill Campbell was not on her own list when she was on community nursing duties, a different nurse visited him. Both Bill and Maria had been more relaxed after Kyle's visit to them, thankful that Penny had not been there since. Alex hoped that would last.

Whilst things remained awkward between herself and Kyle, especially after that moment in his room—an incident to which neither of them had referred again—Alex sensed a change in him. True, he didn't seek her out, he remained wholly professional at work but, while still reserved, the hostile edge that had marked her interactions with him that first week had gone. She remained acutely aware of him, and she couldn't help but worry about him. His words played over and over again in her head and she fretted about his pain, confusion and the sense of betrayal he had been unable to conceal. She also thought with anger and disbelief about the actions of his ex-wife. No wonder Kyle felt rejected, betrayed and found it so hard to trust in anyone again.

Did he mean to bury himself in work for ever? Part of her wanted to discuss the situation with Hannah but she was loathe to divulge Kyle's feelings to anyone, even one of his closest friends. It would be a breach of his trust and confidence. But she was also concerned about the strength of her own feelings for Kyle, and didn't want to have to explain those away to Hannah. Or anyone. She couldn't even explain them to herself. All she knew was that she reacted to Kyle as she never had to anyone else, and the urge to help him was too strong to resist. What she didn't know was how to achieve that aim.

When an opportunity arrived on the Friday of her fourth week at Glenside, she knew it was a big risk, that it may backfire on her and make Kyle angry, but the chance was too tempting to miss. She had stayed back with Kyle after surgery had finished to run the regular well-woman clinic, a drop-in service run on an informal basis and which presented various problems and issues.

'My husband and I are new to the area. We moved here for his job,' Alicia Martin explained, her hands clenched nervously in her lap. 'He… We want to think again about starting a family.'

Alex noted the hesitation, the way Alicia had changed 'he' to 'we,' and wondered if the young woman was feeling under pressure from her husband. In her early twenties, she seemed unusually edgy, and Alex glanced at Kyle, remaining in the room in case her help was needed.

'And is that what *you* want, Alicia?' Kyle asked, clearly picking up on the same feeling she had experienced.

'Yes. No. I'm not sure,' the woman fretted, tears welling in her eyes. 'I'm scared.'

Sitting down next to her, Alex offered her a tissue. 'Scared of having a baby? Of being a mother?'

'We tried once. Two years ago. I lost my baby. I had a miscarriage at eleven weeks.'

The emotion-filled words hung in the air. Suddenly the room was thick with tension and Alex couldn't help glancing at Kyle, seeing the pain in his eyes, the way he tried to distance himself, his body rigid, a muscle pulsing along his jaw. Aching for both patient and doctor, Alex took a breath and stepped in.

'That must have been an appalling experience for you and your husband.'

'I'm not sure I'm ready to try again.' Alicia shredded the damp tissue between her fingers. 'I still can't forget what it was like. I still miss my baby. What if it happens next time? I couldn't do it.'

Alex nodded, understanding the young woman's concern but eager to reassure her. 'Just because you've had a miscarriage once, it doesn't automatically mean you will have another one.'

'I feel it's my fault,' Alicia whispered, reaching for another tissue.

'It is *not* your fault, Alicia. No one is to blame. You have nothing to feel guilty about.' Alex knew she was talking as much to Kyle as to their troubled new patient, and she tried to draw him into the conversation. 'Isn't that right, Dr Sinclair?'

His dark blue gaze fixed on her and Alex swallowed, unable to judge his mood. 'Yes. Yes, that's true. We often have no explanation for why these things occur,' he allowed, his voice rough.

'The figures show that one in four pregnancies ends in miscarriage, and there could be all manner of reasons for it to happen quite beyond your control,' Alex continued, nervous as she wondered how Kyle was reacting. 'Sometimes, as hard and cruel as it seems, it is simply nature's way. It is painful, unfair and deeply distressing, but it is no one's fault.'

'People keep telling me I should snap out of it, move on…forget. I'll never forget,' Alicia stated on a sob.

Alex reached for her hand. 'Of course you won't. And no other child will replace the one taken from you. There is no time limit on grief, Alicia, no right or wrong, only how you feel. You are bound to experience all manner of emotions, from guilt to anger to isolation, and everyone has different needs, different desires about whether to have another baby straight away or never to have another. Everyone recovers or reaches acceptance at their own pace. Your baby will always be in your heart but in time, when it is right, you'll be able to try again if that is what you and your husband want, together. But that's a decision only you can make.'

'I don't feel I ever had closure,' the woman explained now, wiping her damp cheeks with a tissue, and out of the corner of her eye Alex saw Kyle stiffen, as if the sentiment resonated with him too. 'One minute the baby was there, the next it was gone. There was nothing to see, nothing to do.'

'One thing you could think of doing is having a small ceremony.' Alex glanced at Kyle as she made the suggestion, seeing the bleakness in his eyes mixed with confusion and what she feared was a thread of anger.

Alicia cleared her throat. 'A ceremony. Like in a church or something?' She frowned, indecision in her voice.

'No, it doesn't have to be anything like that. Just you and your husband. Or alone, if that is what you need,' she added, pressing on, willing Kyle to listen, to understand. 'Whatever you are comfortable with. It's a way of saying goodbye, of coming to terms. You can get a special box and put things in it—something you bought for the baby, a photo from a scan, if you had one.' She paused for a moment, scared that had been too personal for Kyle. Avoiding his gaze, she ploughed on. 'You can even write a letter telling your baby how you feel, that you will always love him or her. Anything. Either you can put the box away to keep for the future, or you can bury or burn it. Whatever feels right for you. But it's a way of letting go, of accepting the awful thing that has happened to you, that it isn't your fault, there is nothing you could have done differently to change things. You'll never forget, but you can go on.'

Silence filled the room after she had spoken. Alicia sat quietly, apparently lost in thought, but Kyle had turned away from her, his hands gripping the arms of his chair so tightly that his knuckles whitened. Alex wished their patient wasn't present so that she could go to him, comfort him, hold him—but she didn't dare, frightened she had already gone too far, taken too big a risk in pushing him, challenging him to confront his emotions.

When the tension became so thick Alex thought it would suffocate her, Alicia shifted and managed a watery smile. 'Thank you, you've helped a lot. I think my husband and I need to talk much more about our feelings, maybe have a little ceremony or something as you suggest, and then make some decisions about where we go from here. Dr Sinclair, perhaps my husband and I can come back together and see you again when we're ready, just to check things are OK?' Alicia finished, looking and sounding stronger, more determined.

'Yes, of course.' Kyle's voice was uneven, and Alex found her heart was thudding as he turned, still not looking at her, offering Alicia a semblance of a smile as the young woman rose to her feet.

'Thank you again—both of you.'

As Kyle murmured something, Alex showed Alicia out, nerves jumbling in her stomach as she walked back down the corridor. Should she go and talk to Kyle, explain herself? She peeped in at his door but he had swung his chair round, his back to her, and she could just glimpse the scan photo back in his hands. Tears pricked her eyes. She would leave him be, to think. Hopefully he wasn't so angry with her that he would sack her. Creeping away, she tidied everything up and then collected her belongings. Hesitating again, feeling cowardly, she called out goodnight and let herself out of the surgery, facing a lonely journey home in the dark, more worried about Kyle left alone with his painful memories.

Thoughts of Kyle plagued her the next day, and she felt edgy as she went about her chores. It had only been three months since she had lost her father—three months, one week, four days…not that she was counting. But she realised there were all manner of things she, too, had been putting off, unable to face dealing with, like sorting out his clothes, deciding what to do with his possessions, carrying out necessary improvements to the house. It wasn't easy. It affected her deeply just seeing his empty chair by the fire in the living room. This house had been home all her life, where she had always felt loved and cherished and understood, a place that had been a sanctuary for both her father and herself when her mother had died and they had drawn closer together, needing each other.

She could start with small things, like throwing out the old threadbare carpet in the L-shaped hall and exposing the gorgeous slate tiles that matched those in the kitchen. The walls needed painting too. It would be easier dealing with the hall before tackling any of the rooms. She already had the tins of paint, it was a matter of getting on with the job. Her decision made, she set to work, her emotions all over the place as both her father and Kyle continued to occupy her mind.

Her stomach was rumbling, complaining she had put off lunch long enough when she heard the sound of a car arriving outside followed by a door closing and footsteps approaching the front door which she had left open to ventilate the smell of paint. Frowning, she set down her paint brush as the bell rang and walked round the corner to discover the identity of her unexpected visitor. Her eyes widened and her heart pounded as she found herself looking at Kyle.

Why on earth had he called in at her house? She tried to judge his mood, but his fathomless blue eyes revealed none of his thoughts. A myriad emotions churned inside her, and she stifled a groan when she realised what a mess she looked. Just great. Unlike Penny, who always managed to look glamorous, even in her uniform, she herself never looked as polished. Now Kyle had to see her in raggy old jeans and a paint-spattered, shapeless shirt. It could have been worse, she told herself wryly; at least she wasn't wearing her fluffy pink pig slippers! Aware she had streaks of paint on her face, and the unsightly bandanna she had tied over her hair for protection, she met Kyle's deep blue gaze, embarrassed and nervous. She saw momentary amusement there and, to her surprise and alarm, what looked suspiciously like a brief flash of masculine interest. Oh help. It was far better when she was worrying whether he was angry enough to sack her.

'I—' Words failed her and she stammered to a halt. 'Hi.'

'Hi. I hope you don't mind me dropping by.' The deep, husky voice had its usual effect, setting her blood racing in her veins and bringing a tight knot of desire to her stomach.

'No. No, of course not.' She felt ridiculously flustered and uncertain. 'What can I do for you?'

He regarded her for a few moments in silence, as if trying to remember himself why he had come. Sighing, he ran the fingers of one hand through his hair, dislodging a couple of wayward locks which fell across his forehead. 'I wondered… Hell, Alexandra, I don't really know. I just needed to talk,' he admitted, such confusion and loneliness in his voice that her heart melted and it was all she could do not to fling her arms around him and hug him tight.

'Sure.' She stepped back to let him inside. 'Sorry about the mess. And the paint fumes. I was just about to stop for lunch. Have you eaten?'

'No.'

'Then come through,' she invited, alarmed at the shakiness of her own voice, and the awareness curling through her as the house seemed to shrink with the intimacy of Kyle's presence.

As Kyle squatted down on the slate-flagged kitchen floor to introduce himself to Max, her father's elderly Border collie, Alex washed up and fussed around preparing them something to eat. Questions chased through her mind.

Why had he come?

What did he want to talk about?

How long could she manage to hide how she felt about him?

CHAPTER SIX

KYLE attempted to keep his focus on the dog but couldn't stop himself watching Alexandra as she moved around the kitchen. She looked amazing. Aside from the smart but correct suit she had worn to the interview, he had only ever seen her in her nurse's uniform. Today she was grubby and tousled, wearing old clothes and no make-up, but to him she had never looked more lovely. She was always so natural and unaffected. He loved that about her. A total contrast to Penny, with her lashings of make-up and constant preening, self-absorption and cloud of sickly, cloying perfume. Alexandra never seemed to consider herself at all, which was wonderfully refreshing. Right now she looked adorable in her work clothes, a few streaks of lemon-coloured paint on her flawless skin, her grey eyes darker than usual as she turned to face him. The brushed plaid shirt, knotted at her waist, was baggy and hid her luscious shape, as her uniform always seemed to, but those jeans… Wow!

His gaze slid down and his mouth went dry. Long legs encased in faded denim that had to have been sprayed on, the way the material lovingly hugged the rounded swell of her rear and moulded the curves of her thighs. This was not some skin-and-bone model but a real, honest-to-goodness, flesh and blood woman. Alexandra was totally feminine, totally sexy. He could feel the rapid thud of his pulse, and was sure she must hear it, but he couldn't drag his gaze away. He noted a few frayed rips in the soft denim which afforded a tantalising glimpse of golden skin, and he nearly moaned aloud in protest when her fingers unknotted the ends of her shirt and shook it out so it dropped halfway to her knees, cutting off his delectable view. Trying to blank the hunger that must be reflected in his eyes, his gaze slowly slid back up to meet hers, finding her flustered and nervous, even white teeth nibbling the sultry fullness of her lower lip.

He wanted to do that—he ached to kiss her, to taste her, to nibble her all over. This was ridiculous. Straightening, irritated with himself, he shoved his hands into the pockets of his jeans and tried to get his wayward thoughts back under control. For the last eighteen months, since the pain of everything had overtaken him, he had focused on work and lived like a monk. Now, when he least expected it and least wanted it, his libido had returned with a vengeance—for a woman who, by all accounts, had a fiancé cooling his heels in England and who was also possibly juggling a local boyfriend as well. Someone, somewhere, was having a laugh with his life.

'Home-made soup and bread OK?' Alexandra asked, looking self-conscious as she pulled the bandanna off her head and released the short, springy waves of dark blonde hair from their confinement, ruffling the strands with her fingers.

'Sounds good, thanks.'

Wanting to know if her hair was as soft and silky to the touch as it looked, Kyle resisted temptation, watching as she turned away and set a pan to heat on the Rayburn before cutting slices of fresh granary bread, setting them on a plate on the table along with some cutlery, glasses and a jug of water. Now he was here he didn't know what to say, couldn't even explain how he had found himself at her door, driven to come by some unconscious need to be with her.

'Please, take a seat,' she invited him politely.

Feeling awkward and uncertain, he took off his well-worn leather jacket and hung it over the back of one of the wooden kitchen chairs before sitting at the table, helping himself to water. 'Any news of the injured cat you found?' he asked after a moment, eager to break the electric silence that was growing uncomfortably between them.

Leaning against the worktop, she smiled. 'Yes. The x-ray showed he'd broken the hip joint, probably after being knocked by a car. Alistair did an operation and removed the femoral head—you can do that in cats, because they're so light and they manage really well without a proper joint. The cat was neutered and I brought him home within a few days, since when he's been slowly finding his feet and settling in with the assorted cats outside. He's still very wary and shy of people, but he's eating well and hardly limping at all now.'

'That's great.' Her smile did crazy things to his insides, warming places he thought had frozen for ever. 'I'm sorry again for interrupting your decorating.'

'I was glad of an excuse to stop. It's not one of my favourite jobs.'

The admission was accompanied by an endearing wrinkling of her nose that made him smile. 'Have you much to do?'

'A fair bit. The whole house is looking tired, but frankly I've been putting DIY jobs off.' She paused, her eyes darkening, her voice husky with emotion. 'I haven't been able to face all the changes, the tidying up and sorting of things I have to do since my father died.'

'I can't imagine what it must be like, not having parents still around.'

'It was just Dad and me for so long after my mother died

when I was still a child. We were very close, and I miss him. So, tell me about your parents. You said they had a farm?' she asked, clearly trying to lighten the mood.

He saw the suspicion of moisture filming her eyes before she turned back to stir the contents of the pan on the hot plate, a delicious aroma teasing the air. Kyle swallowed, hating to think of her sad and hurting. 'In Ayrshire, yes. I grew up there. The farm has been in the family for three generations. It's dairy mostly, although my parents and brother have been diversifying more of late, what with things in farming being so difficult right now.'

'Did you never want to be a farmer?' She glanced over her shoulder, a glimmer of mischief lightening her expression and all but kicking him in the gut.

'I enjoyed the life, but I couldn't imagine myself doing it full time. Which was just as well as my older brother, Graeme, was far keener than me, and the place couldn't have supported all of us.'

She nodded and took a sip of water. 'So you went to medical school. That must have been a struggle.'

'Financially it was,' he admitted, shocked anew at how easy it was to talk to Alexandra.

'And that's where you met Conor?'

'Yeah.'

They had been two young men out to take on the world for the first time and eager to have some fun, Kyle recalled with a wry smile. Only both of them had struggled for money, and all their time and energy had been consumed working every moment on their studies and in various jobs to pay their way. Conor's family background had been unstable, while his own parents had little spare cash to help him, so he and Conor had needed to earn their keep. They had also shared a flat, shared food, clothes and anything else needed to keep them going and see them through the years of training. As for fun… Well, any oats sown had been a mere handful and not very wild ones because Conor had found himself a steady girlfriend—who'd subsequently dumped him just before they qualified—while for Kyle there had been some casual dates but there had always been Helen waiting in the wings.

Kyle halted his reverie as Alexandra moved to the table and ladled out two bowls of steaming, fragrant soup and then set the pan aside before pulling out a chair across from him and sitting down. 'Thanks for this, it looks and smells amazing.'

'I hope it tastes as good.'

'Better,' he reassured her after his first few spoonfuls.

Smiling, she passed him the bread, then took a slice for herself. 'I'm afraid it's a bit of pot luck with me whether things turn out to be edible or not! Cooking isn't my forte.'

'I'm just in awe how you find time to do everything,' he admitted with genuine appreciation and a hint of concern. 'You said you have help here?'

'Mmm.' She dipped some bread in her soup and popped it in her mouth, the tip of her tongue brushing across her lips, sending a lick of fire through him. Hell. Get your mind out of the gutter, Kyle, he berated himself, looking down to concentrate on his food. 'Jim Buchan lives in one of the old farm cottages along the road. He was a stockman on the estate but had to retire some years ago, and since then he's been helping my Dad out and now me. If there are any heavy jobs to be done outside or in the house, though, I call on Drew.'

A sick weight of dread settled in his stomach and he wondered if Penny's warning had been genuine after all. 'Drew Grainger?' he asked, hoping his voice sounded casual and betrayed none of his inner turmoil.

'That's right. I guess you come across each other through work occasionally. He and Nic have been good friends since they met under a lorry a couple of years ago, rescuing a child in a pushchair. I wasn't here then but I heard all about it.'

'Hannah wasn't best pleased at the chance Niç took.' Kyle recalled the incident, trying to take his mind off the raging disappointment and resignation at the thought of Alexandra being involved with someone. He was a fool, but he had to know. 'I heard you were seeing Drew.'

'Seeing him?' Alexandra looked up, momentary confusion clouding her eyes as she stared at him, then realisation dawned. 'You mean dating or something?' She took him by surprise and burst out laughing. 'Oh, that's a good one! Wherever did you hear that? I can't wait to tell Drew, he'll have a fit!'

'So the rumour mill is a tad off,' he muttered, unwilling to admit how much he wanted to hear her say yes.

'A giant tad!' Another laugh bubbled free, teasing his nerve endings, then she sobered. 'Drew's been my best friend and honorary brother since kindergarten. We sat next to each other in class all through junior and senior schools, too, and we go out sometimes, for a meal or to the cinema, as mates do. He's always done things round the place to help my Dad, and he was a godsend when Dad was ill, sitting with him, helping me, then getting me through the darkest days when Dad died.'

Kyle felt a wave of relief overwhelm him, not only that Penny had been wrong and his stupid, uncharacteristic jealousy had been for nothing, but also that Alexandra had had such a good friend to support her through the most difficult of times. He'd come to doubt his own instincts after the things Penny had told him, but he knew now he had been right about Alexandra... Although he still didn't know the facts about the fiancé.

Their meal finished, Alexandra cleared away the things. 'Would you like some coffee?'

'If you're having some, thanks.'

'Shall we take it outside and enjoy the autumn sunshine?'

Nodding, Kyle rose to his feet. 'I'd like that.'

She poured their drinks into mugs. He followed her as she went back through the house and into a surprisingly large but cosy living room which had a huge fireplace on one side and picture windows along the other, making the most of the stunning rural views. Alexandra slid open a patio door and led the way out to a rustic veranda that ran the length of the house. The garden was overgrown but in a wild and attractive way, bordered by thick native hedges, and filled with shrubs, herbaceous plants and a rampant honeysuckle that still had a few late blooms lingering on it. A couple of goldfinches balanced on the pincushion heads of a stand of teasels, feasting on the seeds, seemingly unconcerned at the human presence. Beyond the hedges he could see across the fields to the woods and hills. It was totally peaceful and he felt a new calm seep into him, as if just being here settled something inside him.

'This is great.' Kyle smiled as he sat next to her on an old but sturdy wooden swing-seat suspended from chains, setting it into gentle motion with a push of one foot.

Her answering smile was reminiscent. 'Dad made it for me when I was about fourteen. I've always loved to sit out here at night and watch the bats, listen to the owls, stare at the stars or just curl up in summer to read a book.'

She cupped her mug in her hands, and Kyle found his gaze lingering again. He had a thing about Alexandra's hands. Well, he had a thing about every bit of her, but her hands fascinated him—short nails, no polish, but well cared for. Her fingers were graceful, slender yet strong, sure but gentle. Watching her tend patients with such care and attention put all manner of unwanted and inappropriate thoughts in his mind, including what those hands would feel like on his skin, her fingers exploring his body and… Damn!

'So,' she murmured into the silence as he battled his runaway erotic thoughts, her voice soft with understanding. 'Are you ready to tell me why you are here?'

He wasn't sure he would ever be ready. He was close to Nic, Hannah and Kate, had let them into his life, but he had only really shared his real self, his thoughts and feelings, with Conor. Now, no matter how much he fought it, he felt an instinctive bond of trust with Alexandra which he couldn't explain even to himself. He felt pulled by an inexplicable temptation to let down his guard and be himself with her. It scared the living hell out of him. She touched him, reached him, in ways he couldn't possibly imagine. And she seemed to understand him instinctively. Unable to resist, he reached out and took one of her hands in his, surprising himself by how much he needed the contact, relieved when she didn't pull away. Instead, she automatically linked their fingers, her skin feeling soft and warm against his.

'I was thinking a lot about what you said to Alicia Martin at the surgery last night.' He cleared his throat, trying to banish the rough edge of emotion that always gripped him when he thought of his lost child. 'The doctor part of me knows you are right, that no one is to blame, these things do happen, that I couldn't have done anything different to change the outcome for the baby, but…'

'But all the medical training in the world means nothing when the event is personal to you,' she finished when his words trailed off, in tune with his thoughts again in that way she had that was at once spooky yet comforting.

He let out a huff of breath. 'Yes.'

'I know. I felt the same way through Dad's illness. I was a daughter, not a nurse, and must have driven Hannah and Nic insane with my worries. I care deeply about all my patients, but things that would never fluster me in my work had me in a wild panic when it was happening to my Dad.'

'Exactly.' Kyle gave her fingers a reassuring squeeze. They were quiet for a few moments and he closed his eyes, breathing in the fresh autumn air. A few more crisp nights and the leaves would really begin to turn, firing the landscape with golds, bronzes and reds. 'That technique you mentioned, the idea about the ceremony and writing a letter, where did that come from?'

'It was something I picked up at a previous job. I've seen it work for people who have suffered a loss of some kind. I think you should consider trying it.'

'Yeah. Maybe. I was thinking that, too.'

As he choked up again, her fingers returned the pressure of his. 'Guilt is a natural part of the grieving process, Kyle. I feel it too, wonder if there were things I could or should have done differently. We beat ourselves up over things beyond our control. But it wasn't your fault, you are not to blame,' she insisted, her voice thick and unsteady.

'I tried to understand, to do the right thing for Helen.'

'Helen made her own choices. Hurtful ones, wrong ones,' she told him, soft but firm. 'You're not responsible for someone else's feelings or actions.'

'But…'

Her hand tightened again. 'It was a terrible time, but it was your loss too, and you had needs. Was Helen there for you?'

Kyle struggled with a welter of mixed emotions ranging from an urge to defend Helen—though he really didn't understand that—to anger and resentment, from confusion to hurt. He had pushed all his own needs aside, had buried himself in work so he wouldn't think, and his whole life had slipped more and more beyond his control as he had felt isolated and lost in his marriage as it crumbled around him. Talking with Alexandra made some things clearer in his own mind, but also raised so many issues he hadn't begun to face or acknowledge.

He had opened up to her more than to anyone, even Conor, exposed an inner part of him he had always kept protected, and he didn't know how he felt about that. Part of him wanted to spend more time with her but part of him wanted to retreat, scared to trust, loath to leave himself open to more rejection and betrayal.

With more reluctance than he wanted to admit, he released her hand. 'I guess I'd better let you get back to your decorating.'

Alexandra said nothing, just took his mug from him, rose to her feet and went back into the house. He felt like an idiot, as if he'd done something wrong. But there was no judgement in her expression when he joined her in the kitchen.

'It's really lovely here.' He filled the silence, not wanting to part on an awkward note.

'It is.' A cautious smile curved her mouth. 'Would you like to have a quick look round before you go?'

His good intentions to put some much-needed distance between them weakened in the face of the temptation to linger. 'Yeah, I would. If you have time.'

'Sure.'

Pulling on his leather jacket, he waited for Alexandra to be ready then, with Max ambling outside after them, they went through the porch off the kitchen into the yard. He enjoyed the tour, some of the panic and urgency that had led him to flee slipping away again as he looked over her stock with a practiced eye, seeing what a good job she and Jim were doing with the place. He closed the barn door behind them and walked beside Alexandra past a well-tended vegetable plot where winter crops remained. When they came to the next enclosure they stopped, leaning on the fence to watch the chickens scratching about as Alexandra tossed them some extra corn.

He'd really enjoyed hearing her talk about the farm, realising how much she loved this place. She was a remarkable woman, he acknowledged, some of his edginess returning as his awareness of her increased again. Not only was she a first-class nurse but she was knowledgeable and genuinely loving of this land which had been her home since birth. Somehow she juggled her life to keep all the balls in the air at the same time, still putting other people before herself. On top of which she had a natural inner beauty that had drawn him from the first moment they had met.

Unsettled by his thoughts, by the very fact he had come here today yearning to be with her, to talk to her, he focused on the poultry. None of the hens took the slightest notice of the cockerel strutting in their midst and, hearing Alexandra sigh, Kyle glanced at her and caught her frown.

'What?' he asked.

'I'm worried about him.'

'The cockerel?'

'Mmm. He's never lived up to his name—Casanova.' Her frown deepened. 'I think he might be gay.'

Kyle couldn't stop the sudden laugh that burst from within him. She was crazy! But wonderful. The laugh felt rusty, and he realised what a long time it had been since he'd done it. Hell, it was a long time since he had done a lot of things, come to that, but Alexandra made him want to indulge in them all: laughter, fun, sex…most definitely sex. Looking into smoky eyes, seeing her bite her lip as she tried to pretend affront at his reaction and not laugh too, he felt the burn of desire flare inside him. The impulse to kiss her was too strong to resist.

One hand rose of its own volition, his palm cupping her cheek, his fingers caressing the warm, silken skin of her neck as he stepped closer. He briefly saw her eyes widen in surprise before his own closed, and he felt a tremble ripple through her as his mouth settled on hers. At last. He lingered a moment, enjoying the feel of her, learning her shape, her taste, struggling to hold on to reality and a shred of common sense. But need overwhelmed him and he couldn't wait another second. Alexandra gasped, her lips parting to his, her arms winding round him, her fingers clutching his back. He angled his mouth more firmly on hers, hearing her whimper as she sank into him, matching his tempo in a slow, deep, drugging kiss that explored with sensual thoroughness.

He felt like a man who had been stranded too long in a desert being given his first drink from a sweet, life-giving oasis. Alexandra tasted divine. The scent of her intoxicated him. Groaning, he took more, demanded more, his free arm wrapping round her, dragging her closer as their tongues teased, tempted, stroked, curled together, drawing into each other's mouths. Dear heaven. Fire streaked through his body and his blood roared in his ears. He nibbled on her, sucked at her, couldn't get enough of her. The kiss turned wilder, rough in its urgency, his fingers sinking into the short strands of her hair to hold her in place even as his other arm tightened further to crush her soft curves against his hardness. He didn't care that he couldn't breathe, that his lungs were burning, that his world was imploding. All that mattered was this heart stopping, unbelievable kiss and the insatiable hunger that fed it.

A helpless noise from Alexandra had a sliver of sanity returning. Dear God, this was going too far—way beyond what he had intended when he had succumbed to the urge to kiss her. Another second and he'd be ripping off her clothes in his desperation to feel her skin. A moment more and he'd be taking her. Here. Now. What the hell did he think he was doing, grabbing her like this, forcing himself on her? What kind of man had he become? Confused, scared at the welter of conflicting emotions inside him—the strength of his need and just how close he had come to losing control and doing something unforgivable—he set her away more roughly than he'd intended, seeing her stumble, her eyes dazed and shocked. Of course she was shocked. She must think he was…well, a lecher or something. Unable to meet her gaze, appalled at himself and his actions, he backed away.

'I shouldn't have done that.' The words came out harsher and colder than he had meant them to. 'Sorry.'

He had to get out of here. Now. He never lost control. Never. Helen had been shy and delicate, reserved when it had come to sex, and it had brought out his protective instincts. He'd understood, had taken care of her, had always been gentle, taking things slowly, frightened of giving free rein to an inner wildness. Alexandra had brought out that whole other side to him, the one he had kept hidden, banked down, unacknowledged and, he had thought, forgotten—a more wildly passionate and adventurous side. It was scary. Alexandra was the only one with whom he had surrendered himself totally. And she had discovered the rawness in him, the rough, untamed passion he'd been unable to contain the second he had touched her. It had been uninhibited, needy, demanding. He should never have done it. He looked at her, stunned, seeing her moist lips swollen from his assault on her mouth, grey eyes wide and dark as she clung to the fence for support, her breathing ragged.

Backing away, he tried to pretend it hadn't happened, but knew he would never forget a kiss that had been explosive, amazing, indescribable. Dangerous. Terrifying. Damn it, how could he have pawed her that way? Whatever must Alexandra think of him? He'd all but attacked her, for goodness' sake. Deeply ashamed, fearful of the unfettered passion raging inside him, he spun on his heel and walked away without another word, unable to trust himself to speak, not to touch her again, tortured by what he had done, and by the side of him he'd been unable to control.

* * *

Alex stared, speechless, as Kyle strode away from her and disappeared around the building. A few seconds later she heard a door bang and his car fire to life. He was sorry. He regretted their kiss. She grasped the fence like a lifeline, her legs too jelly-like to hold her up on their own, her heart hammering, her breath coming in desperate gasps, every atom of her being throbbing and on fire. Shaky fingers rose to her trembling lips as she tried to get to grips with what had just happened to her. She had never, ever been kissed like that in her life. From the moment she had set eyes on him she had thought Kyle had the sexiest mouth on the planet, and it had more than delivered, the incredible kiss so erotic and exciting and, quite frankly, orgasmic that she would have embarrassed them both and melted on the spot given a few more moments.

What had she done? He was her boss, a man she knew was troubled, who was possibly involved with another woman. Yet from the instant his lips had brushed hers she had acted like some shameless hussy, flinging herself at him, devouring the poor man, unable to get enough of him. She closed her eyes, reliving the feel of his body against her, his taste, his mind-numbing kiss, the earthy male fragrance of him. Something had snapped inside her, reawakening her dormant sexual nature, and she had wanted him—badly. The temptation to rip his clothes off, and have her wicked way with him there in her yard, had been almost irresistible. Thank God she hadn't given in. How humiliating that would have been. Bad enough that Kyle had rejected her. He was embarrassed and shocked enough by her behaviour as it was, and the kiss clearly hadn't meant anything to him. He hadn't felt the monumental explosion of passion and desire and clamouring need she had just experienced for the first time in her life.

Alex shivered with awareness and unfulfilled need. Pushing away from the fence, she walked unsteadily towards the house, all too conscious of the yearning ache inside her, the constant throb, the way her nipples had tightened and felt unusually sensitive as they'd brushed against the lacy fabric of her bra. She had wanted his hands there, better still his mouth. She had wanted to feel him everywhere.

Sitting in the kitchen, she buried her heated face in her hands and moaned. She had the sense that, if Kyle was ever shaken out of his rigid control and let down his guard, the outpouring of all that buried energy and need would be shockingly overwhelming and scarily exciting. Untamed sexuality let off the leash. She'd like to find out for herself just how magical it would be with him but she knew she never would. Kyle had brought out a hidden side of her—demanding, needy—but he had been horrified by it and hadn't been able to wait to get away from her.

How was she ever going to face him again?

CHAPTER SEVEN

'I HAD all kinds of plans for my career and where I wanted to be in my life now. I never imagined it would be here, caring full-time for my mother,' John Harrison explained as the kettle boiled. 'Don't get me wrong, I love her and I want to care for her, but there are times I feel so angry and resentful and trapped. Then I feel guilty.'

Alexandra accepted the cup of tea John handed her and waited for him to join her at the breakfast bar in his mother's spacious kitchen. 'Being a carer is a very difficult job, and one that is often unrecognised and unappreciated. It's natural to feel as you do—I see many people who say the same, and often the role creeps up on you unexpectedly. We do the best we can with the cards dealt to us.' She thought not only of John and her other patients but also of Kyle and of herself and the way life had a habit of changing beyond one's control—closing some doors, taking away dreams and hopes, but also opening up others and offering the promise of new opportunities.

'She used to be so active. It's horrible seeing how this osteoporosis has crippled her.'

'I know. Life is very cruel sometimes. Tell me what you originally planned to do,' she encouraged him, resisting the urge to glance at her watch. She knew how late she was, but she sensed John needed this time to let off steam, and listened as he explained the dreams he had been forced to forgo as Libby's illness had taken hold and left her chronically disabled and in pain.

'I doubt I'll ever get to do any of it now.' John's smile was sad. 'So many others will be years ahead of me if and when I ever get back out there again.'

'Have you considered doing some study at home? You can fit it around your caring responsibilities. Studying with the Open University is very rewarding and fulfilling, and if you took some courses now you'd catch up, not have to start from scratch when the time comes. At some point you are going to have to think about and plan for the day you move on with your own life again.'

John frowned, considering her advice, a shimmer of hope in his brown eyes. 'Thanks, Alex. That sounds a really good idea. I'll think about it.'

'I have some information at home. I could bring it next time I visit you and Libby, if you like,' she offered, finishing her drink. 'And they have an excellent website you could browse. If you become a student you can join others on the course forums online, get to know people doing your courses so you don't feel so isolated.'

'You seem to know a lot about it,' he commented with interest.

A wave of memories washed over her as she rose and picked up her bag. 'I cared for my father before he died and I did some home study with the OU myself. I found it very therapeutic and enjoyable.'

It was dark and wet when she left the Harrison house. They had been her last call of a busy day and she was tired, yet she was in no hurry to get back to the surgery. It had been a relief to discover she was needed out on community calls today rather than having to work at Glenside and face the inevitable possibility of seeing Kyle. Heat prickled through her just from thinking of his name. Her lips still tingled, still felt swollen. She could still taste him, still felt drunk on him, could still feel his body against hers, couldn't forget the all consuming, intensely erotic kiss that had rocked her whole being.

She thought back to how he had been that day, before the kiss. That he had sought her out was amazing enough, but that he had talked about his feelings with more openness was promising, especially when he'd admitted he was considering writing a personal and emotional letter to his lost baby as part of the process of saying goodbye, letting go, moving on. But never forgetting. Kyle had seemed more relaxed when they had walked around outside. He hadn't smiled very often, but when he had it had taken her breath away, and to hear him laugh for the first time had been wonderful. The warm, rich sound had been unexpected and infectious, and had touched something deep inside her. It made her wonder what he had been like before the loss of the baby and the break up of his marriage. She would love to hear him laugh more, would love his troubled spirit to allow him that freedom. It had been the laugh, however, that had led to the kiss. Which brought her back to her starting place.

After very little sleep on Saturday night, she had worked like a demon on Sunday, needing the activity to try and put the memory of Kyle and what had happened between them out of her mind. The same as she had attempted today. Not a chance. All she saw in her head was him. Allowed no escape, she relived every second of the kiss in Technicolour detail, her fevered imagination suggesting all the sinfully sexy ways of moving the moment on to its logical conclusion, envisioning her and Kyle twined together in a mating dance as old as time. No! Her knuckles whitened as she clenched her hands on the steering wheel. This madness had to stop. She couldn't allow herself to have those kinds of thoughts about Kyle Sinclair.

She drove slowly back to Rigtownbrae, hoping everyone would have left by the time she reached the practice, but lights blazed from the windows and there were still a couple of cars on the forecourt. One of them was Kyle's. She shouldn't have been surprised; he spent far too many hours working in an attempt to mask his inner hurt and emotions. Sighing, she sucked in a steadying breath, repeating the incessant lecture to herself that she had to see Kyle eventually, and when she did she had to hide her feelings, had to be professional. Somehow. Collecting her things, she went inside and found Lisa Sharpe behind the reception desk in the now deserted waiting area. The plain-speaking Yorkshire woman, who had married Stuart, a local solicitor, twenty-five years ago, was an excellent practice manager—efficient, dedicated and sometimes demanding.

'Hello, Alex,' the older woman greeted her, a strange expression in her watchful eyes. 'Everything all right?'

Puzzled at an undertone she couldn't identify, Alex set her things on the top of the counter and frowned. 'Fine. Why? Is something wrong?'

'I've just had a call from a patient to say you never visited them as expected today,' Lisa explained, shocking her.

'What? But I've done all that were on my list!'

'That's strange.' Eyes narrowed in concentration, Lisa tapped the keyboard and brought up the information on the screen. 'It definitely says here that you were meant to see Deirdre Dunlop today.'

As Lisa tilted the screen so she could see, Alex stared at it in amazement, then drew out a piece of paper from her pocket. 'This is the call sheet I printed off the computer before I left here this morning. Deirdre Dunlop isn't on it,' she informed Lisa, handing it over.

'But that isn't possible.' Lisa studied the paper and looked back at the screen. 'Everything else is exactly the same, just the one entry is missing. What on earth could have happened?'

'I have no idea, Lisa.'

'It's most odd.'

'Problems?'

Alex stiffened in reaction as the familiar, deeply masculine voice sounded behind her, unconsciously shifting away from Kyle as he approached the desk, his focus rigidly on Lisa Sharpe. One brief sight of him was enough to have all her hormones in turmoil, fire licking through her veins, her breath freezing in her lungs.

'There was a discrepancy on Alex's home-visit list today and we were just sorting it out,' the practice manager explained with customary directness.

'What happened?' Kyle asked, moving closer.

Alex concentrated on trying to breathe and not look at him, allowing Lisa to outline the unsettling and inexplicable error between the list on the computer now and the list she had taken that morning. It was very peculiar, but she was methodical in the way she worked and she knew for a fact that she had not missed anything and the call to Deirdre Dunlop had not been recorded before she'd left the surgery. Feeling Kyle's attention switch to her, she steeled herself to remain calm and not slide into a puddle at his feet.

'How do you explain it, Alexandra?'

'I can't.' She fought to ignore the way his low, husky voice hummed right to her nerve endings. 'I have no idea how this could have occurred.'

Kyle shook his head. 'It doesn't make any sense.'

'No. However, the fact remains that Deirdre has missed her visit and needs to have her dressings changed. Lisa, can you give her a ring and tell her that I'll call in to see her before I go home?' Alex asked, picking up her things again and turning to go to the nurses' room.

'You're planning to go now?' Kyle queried, midnight blue eyes dark with confusion.

'Yes, of course,' Alex insisted. 'The cellulitis in both her legs is improving and she's responding to the antibiotics, but she can't be allowed to remain uncomfortable. It isn't her fault this mistake has taken place.'

She was deeply relieved when Kyle let the subject drop and failed to follow her down the corridor. Breathing space, that was what she needed to keep between them. Having sorted out her things, made up the notes on her day's visits and ensured she had what she needed for Deirdre Dunlop's dressing changes, she was preparing to head back out again when Lisa appeared at the door.

'I've spoken to Deirdre and she is very grateful. It's good of you to do this before you go home,' the older woman praised.

'It's the least I can do. I just can't understand what went wrong.'

Lisa frowned. 'No, nor can I. I'll run some tests tomorrow. It may be a good idea if we double check the lists together for now, just until we discover what happened. Hopefully it will be a one-off blip.'

'I hope so too, but I agree that we should get together to compare the schedule.' Alex was pleased at the suggestion while hating the need for caution. Better to have a witness and verify the information just in case further problems occurred.

'Is everything all right with you and Kyle?'

The surprise question nearly gave her heart failure. 'Excuse me?'

'I thought things seemed a bit strained between you.' Lisa watched her with interest, and Alex prayed she wouldn't blush. 'I know Penny has been difficult and given you a hard time since you joined us, but I wouldn't take her too seriously, and she certainly isn't representative of the rest of us. We're all delighted to have you here, Alex.'

'Thank you. I'm glad to be here.' The brisk woman's genuine comment warmed her.

'Penny's nose is out of joint because you and Kyle are clearly attracted to each other.'

Oh, hell! Lisa's perception and uncharacteristic teasing shocked her. 'I beg your pardon?'

'I'm all for it,' the woman persisted, undaunted. 'It's time he started living again.'

'But there's nothing going on! I'm not attracted to Kyle,' she lied, hoping her laugh was convincingly dismissive as she instinctively tried to protect him from gossip and Penny's wrath, even while emotion churned inside her. Her body was going into meltdown as she thought again of their heavenly kiss and what it would be like to repeat it…to go further.

Alex squeezed her eyes shut. *Stop it, stop it, stop it.*

Kyle froze in his progress down the corridor as he heard Alexandra's voice coming through the open doorway. Damn it! Bitter disappointment curled in his gut. He'd been going to apologise to her for his behaviour on Saturday and check she was all right about doing the late home visit, but he'd give it a miss now. No way was he going in there to face her, with her rejection ringing in his ears. What had Lisa said to make Alexandra issue such a vehement denial? Why were they discussing him?

Returning to his consulting room, he slumped down at his desk. Alexandra cared about people. He shouldn't read any more into her kindness to him than that, could only hope she had not been driven by a sense of pity. He cringed at the thought. Whatever her motivation in listening to him, she wasn't attracted to him. She'd been clear enough, for goodness' sake. And he should be pleased, given his own promise to himself that he would never become involved with a woman again. But he wasn't pleased. He may have been in the wrong instigating it, but he hadn't been able to forget their hotter-than-hot kiss on Saturday for a second, and he'd been weakening to the temptation to spend more time with her, see where things went. Now he knew. They were going nowhere. Which was probably just as well. At least he'd not made a fool of himself already and asked her out only to have her refuse. No loss of face. What he had to do was to forget about her, he chastised himself, running his fingers through his hair in agitation. But it didn't change how he felt, didn't stop him thinking about her, wanting her. Damn it!

'Kyle?'

'What is it?' The hurt surprise on the practice manager's face registered through his inner turmoil. 'I'm sorry, Lisa, I didn't mean to snap at you.'

'Is something wrong?'

'No. I just have something on my mind,' he admitted, hiding a sarcastic laugh at himself.

'I was just going to let you know that Alex and I have arranged to monitor the call schedules for the time being while I investigate what happened today.'

'Fine. Keep me informed, please,' he requested. 'I don't want patients or staff being inconvenienced.'

'Alex has gone off now to see Deirdre Dunlop. We're very lucky to have her; she's an excellent nurse and the patients love her.'

Feeling Lisa's gaze on him, Kyle kept his expression blank. 'That's good. You get off home yourself. It's late.'

'Pots and kettles. You work too hard, Kyle. Time to begin thinking about yourself and your own needs again.'

With that parting retort, Lisa left his room and Kyle breathed a sigh of relief. Better still was the knowledge that Alexandra had gone, although part of him was concerned at the hours she was working. Again he thought of how she had been on Saturday…warm, natural, open, sexy as hell. He had never experienced this terrible clawing, craving need for someone before.

Thankfully, his day had been a hectic one with busy surgeries and clinics, and he had been relieved to learn that Alexandra was out on calls rather than at Glenside where he might have had to work alongside her, her presence shattering his concentration. He looked now at the stack of paperwork on his desk which never seemed to decrease—but at least it kept him occupied, kept him from returning alone to an empty shell of a house and, hopefully, would stop him thinking solely about the woman who was driving him crazy. The woman who had stated quite clearly that she wasn't attracted to him and didn't want him.

October had brought late sunshine but November was cold, wet and grey with a hint of the winter to come nibbling in the air. After a hectic Friday morning of consultations, Kyle checked his inbox and found an email waiting for him from Conor.

"We're taking up your idea of a celebratory get-together and are having a dinner for close friends, family and some of our colleagues from the surgery on Saturday week."

Kyle read the information, noting his friends had booked the function room at a renowned country-house hotel halfway between Glentown-on-Firth and Rigtownbrae.

"Kate and I desperately want you to come. Please say yes, Kyle. Nic and Hannah will be there. And if you're free this weekend and fancy getting out on the bikes or for a walk, give me a ring and we'll meet up."

Kyle hit the reply button, fighting the instinctive urge to decline, to keep to himself. But these were his best friends, he cared about them, and maybe everybody was right and it was time for him to begin doing things again. What better occasion than this? Making the decision, he typed a note back agreeing to go to the dinner, and promising to call that evening to fix up a time and place for a jaunt in the hills in the next couple of days. Maybe Nic would be free to come too.

A knock at the door drew his attention. 'Come in.' His heart lurched when he looked up and saw Alexandra hesitate to move closer.

'Sorry to trouble you, I know you've had a busy morning, but I wondered if you could spare a few moments to see a patient.' Wary grey eyes fringed by sooty lashes regarded him, and made him face up to the fact that he had been avoiding her since he'd overheard her words to Lisa on Monday evening. Then there had been the kiss… No, he wasn't going there, he vowed, trying to ignore the way his body reheated and hardened at the very thought of that unforgettable moment. He struggled to concentrate on what Alexandra was telling him. 'Elizabeth is out on calls and Robert is booked solid with the diabetes clinic.'

'What's the problem?'

Looking relieved, she stepped closer to his desk and he leaned forward, fancying he could almost catch the familiar, intoxicating meadow-fresh scent of her. 'Judy Craig is in the treatment room. She came in for a regular health check and cervical smear, but I've spotted what looks to be an unusual mole on her leg and I think it needs further investigation.'

'Is Judy aware of it?' he asked, frowning as he tried to drag his mind back to the task at hand and assimilate what he remembered about the woman—late thirties, married, three children, and she worked as a teacher at the same school as Robert's wife, Lindsay. 'Has she noticed a change in the mole?'

'She said it has been there for years and, although it has been a little itchy lately, she hasn't paid it much attention.'

'OK. I'll come along and see her now.'

Alexandra's spontaneous smile sucked all the air from his lungs. 'Thanks, Kyle.'

He hit the send key to despatch his email to Conor and then followed Alexandra along the corridors to Treatment Room Two, his gaze on her back. Her short hair left the nape of her neck exposed, and it cost him big time to resist the overwhelming temptation to lean in, set his mouth to her and taste the smooth golden skin exposed above the collar of her uniform. Hell, his professionalism was shot to pieces around this woman. Taking a few deep breaths, he tried to get himself back under control as they entered the room.

'Hello Judy,' he greeted, ruthlessly trying to set all else from his mind as he concentrated on their patient. 'I'm sorry you've had to wait.'

'That's all right, although Alex being worried about the mole has made me nervous. Do you really think it might be a problem?' the slim brunette asked with evident concern.

'Let's take a look and see, shall we?'

Judy nodded her agreement, her smile was anxious. 'Whatever you think is best.'

Following Alexandra's directions, he examined the pigmented mole on the back of Judy's left calf. 'I understand you've found it a bit itchy?' Kyle asked, frowning as he looked over the site and saw what had alerted Alexandra.

'Yes, it has been recently, but I never thought anything of it.'

Kyle nodded, suspicious about the irregular edge to the mole and the raised surface. 'Has it changed in shape at all or in colour?'

'Sited where it is, I don't tend to look at it often. It is definitely bigger than it used to be and it does seem darker,' Judy confirmed, twisting her body for a better view. 'Is that bad?'

Kyle glanced up and met Alexandra's solemn gaze, noting the way she stepped nearer to Judy to offer support if it was needed. 'It does make me concerned, Judy, yes, and I think the safest thing is to get it checked out straight away.'

'It's just a bit of a surprise.' She pressed a hand to her chest, brown eyes moist. 'Goodness, to think I never would have given it a notion if Alex hadn't mentioned it.'

'I'll write a letter of referral for you, and you'll get an appointment from the specialist at the county hospital who will do an assessment. He'll likely remove it, take a biopsy and decide what, if anything, needs to be done. Don't hesitate to ask if you have questions and you can get back in touch with us if you need to,' he invited, giving her a reassuring smile.

Looking shell-shocked, Judy straightened her clothes, took an information booklet Alexandra handed to her, and prepared to leave. 'Thank you both very much.'

'No problem.' Kyle offered another smile, moving to open the door for her.

'Ring if you want to talk,' Alexandra added. 'Or come in any time.'

After Judy had gone, Kyle closed the door again and lingered, watching as Alexandra efficiently tidied the room. She never failed to impress him, both with her clinical knowledge and her caring manner with the patients. The ultimate professional, she always put others before herself and she had excellent instincts.

'That was a great call, Alexandra,' he praised her, noting the warm pleasure darken her eyes as she turned to face him. 'You did brilliantly there.'

'Thanks. I hope Judy will be all right.'

Kyle rested his hip against the treatment table and sank his hands into his trouser pockets to stop himself reaching for her.

'So do I. Hopefully it's been caught early—thanks to you. How are things going? Any more problems with the call schedules?' he asked, eager to remain in her company even while an inner voice told him he was a fool.

'No.' A frown replaced her earlier smile. 'Lisa wasn't able to find out what went wrong, but thankfully there haven't been any more problems. Not with house calls.'

'But with something else?' he probed, picking up the underlying edge to her voice.

'I'm not sure. There have been more people failing to show up for appointments at my clinics in the last week.' He watched as she finished her tasks and then sat down. 'I've mentioned it to Lisa and she agrees it is a higher percentage of no-shows than normal… And it only seems to be happening to me.'

The news made Kyle frown too. That did sound peculiar. They had their fair share of missed appointments but on the whole their patients were conscientious and either called to cancel or re-book. He made a mental note to look into the matter and see which patients were failing to turn up. Apart from anything else, he didn't want anyone becoming ill because they were ignoring their symptoms or failing to manage their treatment.

'Lisa is monitoring the situation, and I was going to have a word with you, Robert and Elizabeth so you were aware of any possible issues,' Alexandra continued.

'Thanks. Let me know if you have any other problems.'

'I will.' A pause lengthened and their gazes locked. His gut tightened as Alexandra licked her lips and drew in a deep breath. 'Um, have you heard from Conor and Kate?'

Surprised, Kyle nodded, distracted by her mouth and the memory of how it had felt and tasted under his. 'I had an email from Conor today. We're probably meeting up this weekend, and they're having a celebratory dinner the following Saturday.'

'Yes, I know. I had an invite from Kate.'

'Right.' His own breath seared in his lungs. He hadn't anticipated this eventuality. 'I see.'

'Would you rather I turned it down?'

Her voice was so soft, her expression so wary, that he barely suppressed a groan. 'Of course not! Do you want to go?'

'I'd like to, yes.'

'Then you must.' Alexandra understood him on some deeper level that both calmed and yet scared him, and he was surprised how much he suddenly wanted her to be there when he faced the world again. It wasn't that he needed anyone to hold his hand but, although he'd be amongst friends, he'd not been to any functions in over eighteen months, and as uncomfortable as it was to admit the truth was he had been hiding away. 'Are you going to drive to the hotel?'

Dark blonde waves shimmered as she shook her head. 'No. I planned to ask Hannah and Nic for a lift.'

'You don't have to do that. I'll take you.' The offer was out before he realised what he was doing. Panic set in, yet he couldn't bring himself to retract.

'Are you sure?' Grey eyes widened with surprise and something else he couldn't identify but which brought a burn to his gut. 'You don't have to.'

'I know, but I want to,' he assured her, the nervous excitement curling inside him evidence of how true that was, how tense he was feeling as he waited for her acceptance. He had to remember she wanted nothing more than friendship, no matter how he was coming to feel about her, but he wanted them to spend the time together, even if this wouldn't be a proper date. 'If that's all right with you.'

A flush pinkened her cheeks. 'Yes. Thank you.'

'I'll pick you up about 6.30 p.m. We can sort out the details nearer the time.'

'OK,' she agreed, her voice huskier and less steady than usual.

Feeling relieved, yet edgy and off-balance, he straightened and headed to the door. 'Best get on. Well done again about Judy. See you, Lexie.'

Alex stared at the empty doorway in amazement. She was bemused enough about the turn the conversation had taken, the knowledge that Kyle had actually asked her to go with him to the dinner. Well, not go with him exactly, not as a *date.* But it was far more than she would have expected from him, and the prospect of being with him in any capacity at all fired her blood and fried her brain. It must have done, because she imagined Kyle had just called her 'Lexie'. He hadn't, had he?

She shook her head trying to get a clearer recall of what had happened. Yes, she realised, replaying the last few moments; Kyle *had* said Lexie. No one but her father had ever called her that. But what shocked her most was that Kyle, who had insisted on using her full name ever since they had met weeks ago, had suddenly done the unexpected and used his own shortened version of her name almost like an endearment, his voice deeper, huskier and more compelling than ever. A shiver of awareness rippled through her and her insides clenched with want and longing.

That he should call her Lexie now, after they had barely spoken to each other all week since the kiss, and Kyle appeared to have been actively avoiding her since Monday night, was even more confusing. Had he just offered to drive her to the dinner out of politeness? Or was there some other reason for his invitation? She had a week to ponder on his motivations, to worry whether she would find someone else in the car come Saturday night, evidence that Kyle had his own date. Penny? She suppressed a shudder at the thought. The last thing she wanted was to find herself playing gooseberry.

But if he arrived alone did that mean they were going *together*…or was he just being kind? Alex knew what she wanted the answer to be, knew that her mind was going to torment her with questions and possibilities for the whole week. Knew, too, that as each day passed and Saturday drew closer the excitement she could already feel unfurling inside her would grow and tighten, and, however much she told herself not to become carried away with impossible fantasies, she wanted more than anything to be with Kyle and for it to mean something. For it to mean as much to him as it did to her.

Come Saturday maybe she would find out.

CHAPTER EIGHT

'I'M SO glad you came tonight,' Hannah enthused as Alex accompanied her and Kate to the hotel cloakroom. 'And with Kyle!'

'He just gave me a lift here, we're not together,' Alex corrected automatically, not entirely sure what they were.

It had been a hellish week at work. Aside from several more unexplained missed appointments, which she and Lisa were going to investigate in-depth in the coming days, there had also been a couple more incidents when patients had raised their concerns about treatment they had received from Penny. "I wish it was always you who visited me. I dread Nurse Collins coming, she is so rude and rough," one patient had confided when Alex had been to her home. Another elderly lady, in no fit state to be out, had changed her home visit to a surgery appointment because she had been so worried that Penny would be the one to call on her. The woman had arrived in the treatment room in pain and near to tears with distress.

Alex had seen and heard enough. She had started making a report, with the permission of the patients involved, detailing incidents of lack of care, rudeness and actual fear and, regardless of how close Penny was to Kyle, Alex was determined to present her report to the three doctors and damn the consequences. All that mattered was the care of the patients, and she couldn't stand back and allow Penny to get away with it, even if that meant upsetting Kyle by exposing Penny. It was all so complicated.

As if those problems had not been enough, she had also been asked to cover the extra Saturday shift because someone—Penny, she had since discovered—had called in sick at the last moment. Right—like she believed it was anything other than part of Penny's game plan to make her life more difficult and attempt to sabotage her attendance at Conor and Kate's celebratory dinner. The last thing she had needed was the call in to work, which meant she had arrived home late with little time to rush through her chores and get ready before Kyle had arrived…thankfully alone…to collect her.

The drive to the hotel had been completed with nothing more than stilted conversation between them. Alex had felt her tension increasing with every passing mile, and it had been impossible to ignore the electricity zinging back and forth which had made her more aware, more nervous, more excited, and more awkward by the second. Gone, it appeared, was the man who had so briefly appeared the week before, the man who had called her Lexie in that intensely sexual way.

'Aren't you going to take your coat off?' Kate teased, jolting her from her reverie.

Unconsciously, Alex wrapped her arms around her waist and shook her head. 'I think I'll keep it on all evening.'

'The hell you will,' Hannah laughed.

'Come on,' Kate giggled. 'I've been dying to see this knockout dress Hannah's been sighing over.'

Alex groaned, recalling the trip she had made with Hannah to Moira Montgomery's select dress-shop the previous weekend. 'I can't believe I allowed you to persuade me to buy this dress, much less that I'm actually wearing it,' she muttered, reluctantly slipping off her coat and handing it over the counter, tucking the ticket in her bag.

'Wow!' Kate let out a low whistle. 'That'll open Kyle's eyes for sure!'

'He's not interested in me that way,' Alex protested with a hint of desperation, knowing it was useless arguing with the pair of them when they had their minds set on something.

Hannah waved the comment aside. 'Fiddlesticks.'

'This dress is far more suited to someone like Penny, who has the figure for it,' she added, scared to turn round and look at herself in the full-length mirror.

'Nonsense,' Hannah dismissed. 'Poison Penny hasn't even got a shape. She's too stick-thin. Look at your gorgeous curves, for goodness' sake.'

Alex wasn't going there. All this time on, Mitchell's frequent hints that she could lose some weight still affected her view of herself. Not that she wanted to think of him, now or ever. She'd had no social life at all since she had left Mitchell and had given up the only stable, long-term relationship she had ever had to return home to care for her father. Mitchell's behaviour on learning of her father's illness had proved how wrong he was for her and how poor her judgement had been. She had shut that side of herself down, and it was only now that she was realising how much she missed male company and the physical side of a relationship. It was her feelings for Kyle that had reawakened her, and yet he was also the wrong man in many ways. Not that it stopped her wanting him with a desperation she had never experienced before, or stopped her caring about him and thinking of him every moment. Her body reacted instinctively whenever she saw him or heard him or accidentally touched him. What she had felt for Mitchell was a pale imitation compared to the feelings she already had for Kyle. It was scary because she knew what a risk she was taking, that she was opening herself up to heartache.

'You look amazing, Hannah,' she praised her now, eager to move the conversation away from herself. 'Has Nic seen your new dress yet?'

A sparkle of wicked anticipation lit the green eyes. 'Nope. I decided to keep it a surprise. I hardly ever wear a dress, much to Nic's disappointment, and, although my green one always blew his socks off, I thought I'd raise the temperature a little…although it will probably get me in trouble!'

The look on her face left Alex in little doubt about what kind of "trouble" she meant, and that Hannah enjoyed every moment of it. Although she couldn't help joining in with Kate's laughter, she experienced a pang of envy. Both Hannah and Kate were so lucky to have found such wonderful, loving, sexy husbands.

'Be thankful you can both wear such deliciously revealing dresses,' Kate sighed, one palm resting on the gentle swell of her tummy. 'I'm starting to show, now I'm into my second trimester. We had to have this dinner now so I can enjoy the dancing while I can still see my feet!'

'You look beautiful,' Alex told Kate sincerely, seeing the glow of her skin, the gloss of her long dark hair, and her brown eyes alive with love and happiness.

Hannah nodded in agreement. 'You're positively blooming.'

'Thanks.' Grinning, Kate linked her arms with theirs. 'Come on, girls, let's get moving and show our guys what we're made of.'

Our guys. Alex sighed, wishing that were true in her case. But she mustn't get carried away on dreams and fantasies. She had never been any kind of *femme fatale*, had never been confident of her looks, was too self-conscious of her generous curves. Nor had she ever owned such a daring dress before in her life, and she flushed with embarrassment at the thought of wearing it in front of Kyle, no matter what Hannah and Kate said. What would Kyle think when he saw it? Would he even notice her?

Kyle was thankful to join up with Nic and Conor in the hotel foyer, hoping that having other people around would stop him doing anything dumb… Like forgetting all about the dinner they were here for and dragging Alexandra off to the nearest available bed to satisfy his ever-growing hunger for her. Yeah, right, like that was going to happen, he mocked himself, recalling their awkward, near-silent journey to the hotel.

He had collected her at the agreed time but she had appeared flustered and harassed—unsurprising, when she had unwillingly admitted she had been called in unexpectedly to work all day and had been rushing around to finish her chores at home and get ready in time. The extra shifts were happening far too often, and he had made a mental note to check into the rosters next week and find out what was going on and why Alexandra was being overly burdened. He feared someone was taking advantage of her dedication and generous nature.

Gauche as a teenager on a first date, he had felt foolishly tongue-tied, and the electric tension had built and built until he had been on the point of explosion. In the dim light inside the car he had only been able to catch glimpses of Alexandra's appealing profile, but the teasing strains of her natural, wildflower scent had slowly seeped into him, increasing his awareness and tightening the fist of need inside him. No matter how much he told himself that they were nothing more than unofficial partners this evening, *friends*, that Alexandra had stated she wasn't interested in him, the growing attraction and the sexual charge between them had been impossible to ignore. For him, at least. Now she had gone off to the cloakroom with

Hannah and Kate, which gave him a few moments to try and get his wayward control back in some kind of order before she returned and he could see what she was wearing for the first time.

'You're wound up tighter than ever,' Conor commented with a wry smile. 'You OK?'

'Fine.'

He was just obsessing about Alexandra day and night. That he thought so much about her was something he refused to acknowledge to anyone, let alone that he dwelt every moment on what it had felt like to hold her, kiss her. And how much more he wanted to do with her.

'You look on the ragged edge, my friend,' Nic agreed, a mix of amusement and sympathy in his voice.

'Yeah, well, it's been a while since I've been out to anything,' he excused himself, knowing it wasn't exactly a lie but scarcely scratched the surface of the torrent of emotion bubbling within him.

Conor rested an arm across his shoulders. 'Kate and I are just delighted you are here to share tonight with us. Speaking of whom, what are the ladies doing in there?' he chuckled, lightening the atmosphere as he glanced towards the cloakroom.

'I am impatient to set eyes on my wife!' Nic admitted, voice husky. 'She has threatened me with a daring new dress and refused to allow me to see it before we left home!'

Kyle couldn't help but smile as Conor gave Nic a consoling pat on the back. 'Just try to behave and not shock everyone before the evening gets underway,' he teased, before his own eyes gleamed with anticipation. 'I replaced the delicious trouser suit Kate was wearing the night of the combined-services dinner back in the spring. It never got an outing because we came across that car accident and it was ruined. She looks amazing in it.'

It was obvious that emotional, Italian Nic couldn't keep his hands off Hannah, his dark eyes burning with desire, while Conor was equally attentive and madly in love with Kate. Kyle was unprepared for the wave of envy that swept over him. It was more than all he had lost with Helen, because seeing his two friends with their wives made him realise all the more that his own marriage had been lacking so much in comparison. What he felt for Alexandra, however…

'Madre del Dio!'

Nic's heartfelt groan interrupted Kyle's thoughts and he saw the flush of colour stain his friend's cheekbones, the Italian's dark eyes narrowing with intent as he took a step forward. Beside him, Conor laughed, and Kyle turned to see what had attracted their attention, his movements halting, his heart stopping, as he saw the three women leave the cloakroom and walk towards them. Kate did, indeed, look stunning in her shimmering one-piece trouser suit, and if Nic's reaction was anything to go by, the green-and-copper dress that clung to Hannah's body, plunged daringly in front and with a slit up one thigh, had already sent him over the edge.

But Kyle hardly noticed because he couldn't drag his gaze away from Alexandra. *Mother of God*. Mouth dry, he silently echoed Nic's heartfelt reaction. The blood singing in his veins, he watched as she stepped forward, her cheeks pink with self-conscious awareness, one hand fluttering down the front of her dress as if in nervous discomfort. The knee-length material clung to her sexily curvaceous frame in a way that surely had to be illegal. It was neither too low at the neckline nor too short in the skirt, and it appeared to cover everything essential, yet it left nothing whatever to the imagination. And he had a *superb* imagination.

Beads of perspiration popped out across his brow. Hell, it was suddenly impossibly hot around here, he fretted, wrenching at the constriction of his tie, his gaze locked on Alexandra. The dress had an irregular solid black pattern over some kind of netted golden background. As she came closer still, the breath hissed out of his lungs and he stared dumbstruck, about to go into meltdown, when he realised that the dress was see-through, and the golden underlay behind the black lacy fabric wasn't cloth at all but Alexandra's skin. Dear heaven. He had to sit down before he embarrassed himself.

Kyle looked delicious in his dark suit, but it was the unexpected fire in his sultry dark-blue eyes that caused the breath to lock in Alex's lungs and set her heart thudding a wild tattoo beneath her ribs. Swallowing, she dragged her gaze from his, standing nervously to one side as she watched Kate and Hannah be claimed by their adoring husbands.

'You look stunning, *cara*,' Nic complimented her, once Hannah had been thoroughly kissed and was tucked possessively at his side.

Alex felt a blush heat her cheeks. 'Thank you.'

Self-conscious, she clasped her bag in front of her, tinglingly aware of Kyle moving closer, his gaze searing her body. Nic and Conor exchanged a knowing look before smiling at her, then turned towards the function room.

'Let's find our places and wait for the others to arrive,' Conor suggested.

It turned out to be a small but select group, and Alex found herself separated from Kyle as introductions were made to the new arrivals. She met Kate's father, Tom Fisher, for the first time and liked him immensely, noting how attentive and clearly smitten he was with Glentown's practice manager, Aileen Nicholson. Some of the other surgery staff were there, including Conor's partner, Dr Fred Murdoch, and Alex was relieved to find them all friendly and welcoming.

Her nerves returned when she discovered she was sitting next to Kyle during the meal. She barely tasted the food, every particle of her being aware of his closeness, the occasional brush of his thigh against hers or the press of his shoulder. The woody, masculine scent of him was subtle yet arousing, and she could feel the heat of his body across the short distance that separated them. It was increasingly impossible to sit still and, however much she struggled to focus on the free-flowing conversation and laughter that rippled back and forth across the table, she became more edgy with every passing moment.

'Are you all right?'

Alex nearly jumped out of her skin when Kyle's fingers met hers under the table, the warmth of his breath caressing her cheek as he leaned closer, the deep, husky voice whispering in her ear. 'Fine,' she managed, her voice sounding strained and different.

Alarmed, she slid her fingers from his and fussed with her napkin, thankful that the meal was nearly at an end. After a toast to Conor and Kate, the music started and couples took to the floor. Alex was surprised when Nic and Hannah appeared at her side.

'May I have this dance, *cara*?' the Italian asked, a twinkle in his dark eyes.

'Thank you.'

Smiling, Alex placed her hand in his and rose to her feet, grateful for the opportunity for some breathing space from Kyle. He, she noted, was being tugged to his feet by Hannah, a reluctant smile curving his impossibly sexy mouth.

'You are enjoying the evening?' Nic asked, ever the gentleman.

'Very much.' Seeing his gaze stray to his wife, Alex smiled. 'Hannah looks beautiful.'

A chuckle rumbled from him. 'She does. To me she is always beautiful.'

Alex almost sighed at the depth of love in Nic's voice, wondering what it must be like to have the kind of partnership he shared with Hannah, and that Conor shared with Kate. To her it seemed they had it all, not just love but respect, friendship, desire, everything. She couldn't help looking at Kyle, a shiver of awareness rippling through her when she discovered he returned her inspection with searing intensity.

Nic spun her round, laughing. 'I think you have turned a certain doctor's head, *cara,* and you are making him realise that life is still worth living.'

'I don't know about that,' she protested, cursing the blush that stained her cheeks.

'You are also finding your feet again after all you have been through, no?' Nic's smile was understanding, his softly accented words making her wish for things she wasn't sure she could have…wasn't sure she should go for even if she could. 'Follow your heart, Alex, you deserve happiness, too.'

'So what's happening with you and Alex?'

'Nothing.' Kyle tried to drag his gaze away from the woman in question and looked at the mischief sparkling in Hannah's eyes. 'Why?'

'You look like you want to drag her off to your cave and devour her!' she teased with a knowing smile.

Kyle shook his head. 'I'm sure her fiancé would love that.'

'Fiancé?' For a moment Hannah looked startled, then her eyes darkened with anger. 'You don't mean Mitchell? Damn it, Kyle, you've not mentioned that man to Alex, have you?'

'No, of course not.' He frowned, wondering what had caused the strenuous response and made Hannah bristle with protectiveness and concern.

'Thank goodness for that. My advice is, don't.'

Which didn't help him a whole lot. Did that mean this Mitchell person was still in Alexandra's life or not? 'What happened?'

'I shouldn't really be telling you, it isn't my place, but just so you don't put your foot in it, I will.' Kyle saw Hannah glance at Alexandra as she twirled round the room with Nic. 'I vaguely knew of Alex when I was younger; we were at the same school but I was a few classes ahead of her. I only really got to know her during the time her father was ill, but we hit it off straight away. You know she moved down to England because Mitchell's job took him down there? She was torn, not wanting to move so far away from her roots, but it was her first really serious relationship and she thought she was in love with him, thought they had a future together.'

Kyle nodded, listening to Hannah, but his gaze remaining on Alexandra, his stomach tightening as he saw her relaxed and laughing with Nic. 'Go on.'

'When her father admitted to her about his illness, she was devastated and never had a thought but to come back to be with him and care for him,' Hannah continued, and Kyle ached for what Alexandra must have been through. 'Mitchell, the creep, gave her an ultimatum. He said if she made the decision to go home, their relationship was over. He wasn't so polite about it, of course. He said some terrible things to her, along the lines that she was choosing some ailing old man on his last legs from her past over her future with him, that if she loved him she wouldn't go.'

'Bastard.' Kyle gritted his teeth, wanting to deck the man who had hurt Alexandra and been so cruel and unfeeling.

Hannah nodded in satisfaction. 'My sentiments exactly. Needless to say, it took Alex all of one second to give Mitchell back his ring and tell him in no uncertain terms where he could go. She packed up straight away, resigned from her job, came home and never looked back. She hasn't heard from him again and has no regrets about her decision, either. She and her father were so close, she gave him everything that last year, devoted herself to him totally, and it hit her so hard when he died.'

Kyle was still absorbing the information when Conor and Kate joined them and they swapped partners. As Conor danced with Hannah, Kyle smiled down at Kate.

'Thanks for coming tonight; I hope it hasn't been too difficult for you.' Her brown eyes reflected her concern.

'Of course not. I wanted to be here.' He discovered the words were true, that, although he still felt the loss of his own baby, the smart of pain had lessened. 'I'm enjoying myself and I'm really happy for both of you. You look fabulous.'

Smiling, Kate brushed a kiss across his cheek. 'It's so good to see you coming out of yourself again. Conor's been so worried about you. We all have.'

Kyle gave Kate a gentle hug by way of answer, looking over her shoulder as Alexandra was handed over to Conor and Nic reclaimed Hannah. He knew it was Alexandra's influence, her presence, that had made him face the things he had been avoiding. She had helped him put events in a different perspective. Whilst he would never forget, he did feel he was beginning to come to terms with the loss of the baby, accept it wasn't his fault, that he couldn't have done more. And, despite his promises to himself, Alexandra made him want to think that a different future might be possible after all.

Another few moments later and he handed Kate back to Conor, his heart thudding as he claimed Alexandra for himself, feeling possessive, aware of the sexual charge that shot through him like an electrical current as he drew her into his arms. He felt a tremor ripple through her as he inched her closer, saw the rosy bloom on her cheeks, the spark in her grey eyes as her gaze clashed with his then skittered away again. He knew that she felt the connection between them too. His body tightened as they moved to the music and he brushed against her, feeling the heat of her skin through the flimsy fabric of her dress. Flexing the fingers of one hand at the small of her back, he pulled her closer still, wishing they were alone, that there was nothing at all between them, wondering how soon it would be before they could leave…and if he could hang on to his fragile control when they did.

Dancing with Kyle was wonderful but terrible. Their bodies fitted together like two halves of a whole, a fact that set her imagination whirling with other things they could do well together. Heat seared through her, and she tried to put such illicit thoughts out of her mind.

It had been a long time since she had been close with a man and, as much as she had enjoyed the physical side of their relationship, Mitchell's kisses had never stirred her to the edge of oblivion like Kyle's had done. Nothing had ever compared to that. Held in his arms, their bodies as one as they moved to the music, she couldn't help but wonder what it would be like to be intimate with Kyle. He was so gorgeous. Every look affected her, every touch branded her his and set her whole being on fire until she was burning with arousal, tense with the strain of trying to hide how she felt about him.

Alex had little concept of time as they danced, talked with their friends and the other guests then danced some more, but, much earlier than she had expected, Kyle suggested it was time to leave.

'Are you sure you don't mind filling in for me and covering my BASICS shift tomorrow afternoon?' Hannah asked, her cheeks flushed, her eyes sparkling.

'I'm positive. I'll be on call from three p.m. as agreed,' Kyle replied with a knowing smile. 'You and Nic hardly ever get time off together. Now you have cover for the patients, someone sitting the animals, and a chance for a night in this secluded hotel… Make the most of it!'

Alex saw Hannah glance at Nic, and noted the look of sultry intent in his dark eyes as he slid his arm possessively around her waist. 'We plan to!' they said in unison.

'It was great that you both joined us tonight.' Conor smiled when they said goodbye to him and Kate. 'Have a safe journey home, Kyle.'

'We will.'

Sensing Kyle was increasingly on edge, attuned to his moods, Alex didn't linger. 'Thank you for inviting me.'

'It's been lovely seeing you.' Kate gave her a hug, pausing to whisper in her ear. 'Have fun!'

Blushing, Alex passed the comment off with a laugh, her insides churning as she headed out of the function room and went to collect her coat. It was clear what Kate had been thinking, but Kyle seemed anxious to leave, clearly keen to drop her off and get back to his own home. She knew this was the first time he had been out to anything in a long while, and maybe he'd simply had enough of socialising for one night. She could understand that. It was a long time for her, too. When she left the cloakroom, Kyle was waiting for her by the door, his body tense.

'Is something wrong?' she asked worriedly.

'No.'

He dragged a hand through his hair, holding the front door open for her before leading the way out to the car park. One of his hands rested at the small of her back as he almost sped her along, and she fancied that even through the thickness of her coat she could feel his touch. When they reached his vehicle, Kyle removed his hand, wrenching off his tie before opening the passenger door.

Aware of the strained atmosphere between them, Alex hesitated. 'Kyle—'

'Get in the car, Alexandra.' Surprised at the roughness of his voice, her gaze clashed with his and, in the reflected glow of a security light, her breath caught as she recognised the darkly sexual heat in his cobalt blue eyes. 'I need to take you home…while I still can.'

The silence inside the car was deafening. As Kyle drove through the dark night, his fingers clenched on the steering wheel, Alex clasped her own hands in her lap to prevent them shaking, positive he must hear every manic beat of her racing heart. Anticipation built inside her. What would happen when they reached her house? Should she invite him in? Would he stay? She wanted him to…wanted him as she had never wanted anyone in her life, was desperate for him to ease the empty ache of need inside her. But she also suspected that Kyle wasn't ready for any kind of commitment, that this would be a one-off moment out of time. Could she accept that? Could she still work with him afterwards?

When they pulled up at her house, Kyle switched off the engine. Still not speaking, they got out of the car, and Alex was sure her legs were too unsteady to carry her as she headed towards the door, her fingers trembling as she tried to insert the key in the lock. Aware of Kyle behind her, she stepped into the hall, hearing his breath hitch as she set down her bag and then shed her coat, hanging it up. Shaking, she turned to face him, pulse racing, trying to be sensible, to give him an excuse to leave.

'Kyle, I—'

Her words ceased as he lifted a hand and pressed two fingers to her lips. Every part of her shivered as his hand slid across her cheek, then her neck, coming to rest at the nape as he held her still. He closed the distance between them, and she felt hot all over as his sultry gaze focused on her mouth, his eyes heavy-lidded. His free hand rested on the flare of her hip, scalding her, drawing her towards him. When his lips brushed hers she thought her breathing had ceased altogether. He teased the corner of her mouth, denying her the kiss she craved, his lips feathering across her face, along her jaw, down her neck, teeth and tongue tormenting her. Her hands rose to his sides to clench in his jacket, trying to keep her balance as she swayed, feeling light-headed from his touch.

'We shouldn't,' she protested weakly, trying to maintain a last fragile hold on reality but unable to think straight while his lips were caressing her skin, now finding a sensitive spot along the line where neck met shoulder.

'We should.'

She smothered a whimper and tried again. 'Kyle… We can't.'

'We can.' His voice was low, husky, persuasive, heavy with need. 'You've been driving me insane all evening.'

Her body quivered as his hands moved, inching up the hem of her dress, fingertips grazing tantalisingly over the bare skin of her thighs above her stocking tops. Just when her legs threatened to give way, and she couldn't stand unaided any longer, he lifted her and she instinctively curled her legs around him to steady herself, gasping as he pressed her back against the wall, making her all too aware of his arousal. *Oh my!* She moaned as his lips settled at the hollow by her ear, teeth nipping, his tongue caressing her before his lips worked their way down to her throat, hot and seductive.

'Kyle—'

'Do you want me to stop?'

Yes, her head screamed. Her last atom of common sense ordered her to speak the word aloud, even as her fingers sank into the thickness of his hair, holding him close as he sucked erotically on her skin, his hips moving rhythmically and oh so suggestively against her.

'No,' she whispered, scarcely able to breathe, unimaginable desire coursing through her, knowing the battle had long ago been lost. 'No. Don't stop.'

CHAPTER NINE

'BEDROOM?' Kyle demanded hoarsely, his breath hot on her skin.

'A-along the corridor. Second door on the right.'

She had barely forced the words out before Kyle was moving, refusing to put her down. She tightened her hold, resting her head on his shoulder, part of her desperate for the will to stop him, scared this was a terrible mistake, the other part of her swept along on a tide of passion the like of which she had never experienced before. It was foolish. She feared Kyle would regret it in the morning, that it didn't mean to him what it did to her, but for now, this magical night, she had to know just once what it was like to make love with him. Her need for him was too desperate to deny any more.

'I'm not on the Pill,' she managed when they reached her room, her voice no more than a rough whisper. 'Have you got anything?'

Swearing, he set her feet to the floor, keeping hold of her as he met her gaze, his eyes tortured. 'Hell. No, I haven't,' he rasped, and she was momentarily glad that he hadn't planned this, prepared for it, expected it.

'My bag.'

'What?'

'My bag.' She pointed across the room to her medical bag. 'I carry a couple of packets of condoms for the young patients I see.'

'Thank God.'

As if he didn't dare to release her in case she vanished in a puff of smoke, he kept an arm firmly around her waist, waiting impatiently while she opened the bag and found what they needed. 'I've got one.'

'One?'

'Sorry?' She glanced at him in confusion, and the look of hungry need in his eyes turned her insides molten.

'The way I'm feeling right now, you'd best grab a good handful—to start with.'

'Kyle!'

Excited anticipation tightened the ache of need inside her as she handed a full box to him with shaking fingers. Heated urgency simmered between them as they began shedding each other's clothes. Her heart lurched when his jacket and shirt were tossed aside and the muted light in the room cast shadows over his impressive physique—all the walking, climbing and mountain biking he did responsible for the lean muscles she now felt under her hands as she explored his shoulders, his hair-brushed chest and tight abdomen. He sucked in a breath as she pressed her lips to one male nipple, teasing him with her tongue, testing with her teeth, breathing in his scent as her fingertips trailed across his taut belly, around his navel and followed the narrow line of hair down to the fastening of his trousers.

Kyle caught her hands. 'Me next,' he decreed, eyes dark with desire.

Her heart ricocheted against her ribs as his hands slid up her arms, making her tingle as he reached round to find the tab of her zip, his breath a warm caress against her face. She quivered as he inched it down and his fingers grazed her bare skin down her spine. Heat flooded through her.

'This dress should be illegal,' he murmured huskily. 'You had me on my knees the second I saw you in it. I've been wanting you all night. Wanting to peel it off, to kiss and touch you all over.'

Alex couldn't remember how to breathe. His words tied her up in knots and then his hands were doing just what he said he had wished to…peeling the clingy, see-through fabric off her body. Once her arms were free, Kyle sank to his knees, and she clutched his shoulders, feeling the flex of muscle as he skimmed the fabric down past her hips and away before he slowly rolled down one stocking and then the other, next deftly disposing of her panties. She couldn't stop shaking at the sensation of his touch on her bare skin, and she gasped, her fingers sinking into the thickness of his hair when he leaned forward and set his mouth to her navel, her muscles tautening as he teased her with his lips, teeth and tongue.

'Kyle…' she moaned, overwhelmed by her body's reaction.

He rose to his feet, and her own fingers moved to unfasten his trousers with more haste than skill, her gaze on his as she eased them down over his impressive arousal, taking his boxers with them. Unconsciously, she licked her lips as she stared at him. *Oh God!* She swallowed, taking in the male perfection of him, her fingers brushing up the outsides of his warm, muscled thighs. He unclipped her bra, tossing it away so he could look his fill. She shifted nervously under his heated inspection, but he caught her hands when she instinctively moved to cover herself.

'Don't,' he chided, gaze hot. 'You're perfect.'

'Hardly! There's too much of me.'

He shook his head in instant denial and reassurance.

'Never. Perfect and beautiful,' he reiterated, smiling as he gave her a gentle push and tumbled her to the bed.

He came down with her, no barriers left between them. After a deep, drugging kiss left them both breathless, he swept her away to paradise as he began a thorough journey of exploration with his hands and his mouth. She couldn't stop the whimpers of need and desire that escaped from her, and she arched off the bed as he lavished attention on her breasts, shaping and caressing one with his hand while driving the other wild with his lips, teasing, nipping, laving with his tongue before suckling the sensitised peak deeply in his mouth.

Alex clenched her fingers in his hair, unable to get enough of him. Nothing had *ever* felt this exquisite, this special, this right. He roamed down her body, setting every particle of her aflame, devoting himself to her pleasure, building her up a plateau at a time until she was writhing beneath him, her hands fisting in the bedclothes as she tried to stay earthed to something. She ought to stop him…but it felt so good.

'Come for me, Lexie.'

She moaned at his dark demand, impatient for him to fill the aching void inside her. 'With you. Please.'

'Next time,' he promised.

His hands held her where he wanted her, and his mouth gave her no respite as he drove her on. She wanted to touch and taste him too, wanted… *Oh, God!* The pleasure had never been this intense. It was unbearable. Wonderful. She couldn't hold on. Her eyes closed and she surrendered herself to the inevitable, sobbing helplessly as she gave herself up, trusting Kyle to keep her grounded, to bring her back, as she was carried away on a wave of unimaginable ecstasy, tumbling in exhilarating free fall as she plummeted over the precipice.

Tremors racked her and she gasped in ragged breaths as Kyle slid back up her body, soothing her. She clung to him, reveling in the feel of his heated skin against hers, the feel of his weight, and she shifted to bring them into closer contact. Gentle fingers traced her face and she managed to force her eyes open, struggling to focus on him, seeing how close he was to the edge, his blue eyes nearly black with fevered desire.

'You are amazing,' he praised, running the tip of his tongue across her lips.

Her mouth opened to his, her hands gliding down his delicious muscled body, learning his textures, his contours. Kyle groaned, breaking the kiss, burying his face in her neck, biting on her skin. Restless, renewed anticipation building inside her, desperate to know him fully for the first time, she watched as he reached out, took a condom from the box and rolled it on.

'Don't wait,' she pleaded.

'Give me a minute.'

Alex sensed he was fighting for control, and didn't want him to. 'Kyle—'

'I want to be gentle with you,' he murmured raggedly, his whole body tense.

'No. Kyle, I'm not fragile. I'm not going to break. You're not going to hurt me.' Her teeth nipped his earlobe before her tongue salved the sting. Her hips cradling his, she moved enticingly against him. 'Let that control go. I want all of you. Everything. Please.'

Her invitation appeared to break through his rigid restraint, allowing him to free the part of him he kept locked away. His hold tightened, and she met his fiery gaze as he groaned and united them with one smooth, searing thrust that had her crying out and clinging to him. She wrapped herself around him, hitching her legs higher and lifting her hips to meet him, taking him completely, as deep as she could. More than once she had wondered what it would be like if all his suppressed sexuality was given free rein. Now she knew. And she gloried in it, in him, stunned and delighted as she met him demand for demand.

The pleasure their bodies found together was overwhelming. She matched his rhythm as together they went on a sensual, erotic journey, their rough passion flaring out of control as they burned down the night, slaking their need for each other. It was beyond anything she had ever imagined. The friction was indescribable, the sense of fullness was intense. She never wanted it to end but she could feel an explosive release building within her, threatening oblivion, refusing to be denied.

'Lexie…'

'Don't stop.' She cried his name, taking everything, giving everything. 'Yes, Kyle, please.'

Clinging together, they tumbled over the edge as one, soaring, flying, riding on a crest of excruciating, impossible pleasure. Hearing her name on his lips as he bound her to him, Alex didn't care if she never came back to earth again as long as she was with Kyle for ever.

Kyle groaned as he shifted, and muscles he'd forgotten he had protested at the movement. A mix of disappointment and concern curled inside him when he fought free of sleep and found himself alone in Alexandra's bed on Sunday morning.

'Lexie?'

There was no answer, no sound inside the house. He glanced towards the window and discovered it was barely light, a weak sun pushing lazily above the hilly horizon. He lay back for a moment, taking stock, remembering the night before. His body immediately stirred in response to the Technicolor memories running through his brain. Last night had been the most incredible experience of his life. He couldn't remember how many times they had reached for each other, the insatiable hunger only increasing, never abating, after he had done as she had demanded and loosened his hold on his control. His long-held fear of indulging in his passionate nature, sparked by Helen's timidity, had been forgotten. With Lexie it had been wild, frenzied, hotter than hot. Smiling, he ran a hand through already tousled hair, hugging her pillow to him, breathing in her fragrance. She had been amazing, uninhibited, giving. Making love with her was like nothing he had known before. Wonderful but scary. Passionate and adventurous. And he was never, ever going to get enough of her.

He threw back the duvet and swung his legs out of bed, needing to find her and allay the sudden anxiety clouding the pleasure. He froze momentarily as his gaze encountered the dog which sat a few feet away by the door, staring silently at him. Max, the elderly Border collie, regarded him curiously. Relaxing, Kyle talked softly to the dog, waiting for its approach, his hands gently soothing over the silken coat, the fingers of one hand rubbing behind the dog's ears. The attention earned him a toothy grin and a lick on a bare kneecap as Max wagged his tail enthusiastically.

'OK,' Kyle murmured, rising to his feet. 'I need to find your mistress.'

After a quick visit to the bathroom, he pulled on his trousers and shirt from last night, pausing as he heard the metallic clang of a barn door outside. With Max leading the way, he walked through to the kitchen, where the smell of fresh coffee teased him, but he needed Alexandra more than he needed his first caffeine fix of the day.

In the large porch by the back door was an untidy collection of boots and a few hooks with jackets and jumpers hanging on them. He found a pair of Wellingtons that fitted, and a shabby but warm fleece that wasn't too small, and he pulled them on before opening the door, scattering an assortment of semi-feral cats as he stepped outside and headed across the yard, his breath misting in the chill November air, his canine companion at his heels. He could hear the soft murmur of Alexandra's voice coming from one of the barns along with the sounds of animals breathing and munching. He let himself in, watching for a moment as she fed the stock, his breath catching at the sight of her, natural and unaffected, wearing old jeans that clung as lovingly to her curves as he wanted to, and a baggy jumper that had seen better days. Her hair was held back off a face left free of make-up, and to him she had never looked more desirable, more sexy. Sucking in a steadying breath, leaving Max by the door, he went to help her.

'Morning.'

'Hi.' Her gaze skittered shyly away from his. 'You don't have to do that.'

He saw the flush stain her cheeks and smiled, wondering how she could be shy after the deliciously wicked intimacies they had shared throughout the night. There were things he wanted to do with Lexie that he'd never done with anyone before. Breaking up a bale, he tossed a wedge of hay into the food trough. 'I enjoy the work. It's been a while.'

She nodded, and he knew she was aware of his familiarity with the stock. 'Jim doesn't come in on Sundays unless I have to work.'

Allowing the silence to stretch, he worked on by her side, opening a new bale and rolling up the twine before adding more hay along the length of the troughs. When the chores were completed he followed her back outside, watching as she let out the chickens, fed them, then gave them fresh water before checking the nest boxes, placing four warm brown eggs carefully in her bucket. Setting it down, she leaned on the fence, looking at the view, and sighed. Grateful for the chance to be able to touch her again—at last—Kyle walked up behind her, moving in close, wrapping his arms around her, spooning their bodies together, and resting his cheek against hers as he gazed in contentment over the rolling fields and hills and woods. The trees showed russets, oranges and reds in the late autumn morning.

'It's beautiful here,' he murmured after a moment, hearing the wistfulness in his own voice.

'I like it.'

'I'm not surprised. It's part of you.' He snuggled closer, breathing in the fresh air and the teasing scent of her skin. 'I always wanted to find somewhere like this to live. Helen and I...'

The words trailed off, uncertainty gripping him, and he was surprised when Alexandra's hands came to rest over his. 'Go on,' she invited softly.

'We'd bought a nice place not far from town, but we didn't have much land and the views weren't as good as this. It had to be sold when we divorced.'

She nodded, her fingers briefly tightening on his, but she didn't offer any platitudes. It was clear she understood, and that meant more to him than words.

'Max disturbed you?'

'No, but he was staring at me when I woke.' A smile curved his mouth and he nuzzled against her. 'Can't say I wasn't hoping to wake up cuddling you, though.'

Again a flush warmed her cheeks. 'The cattle had started bellowing for their breakfast,' she offered by way of explanation, but he couldn't help wondering if she would have stayed with him otherwise. A curl of unease tightened inside him as he sensed her edginess, a distance growing between them. Was she regretting what had happened last night?

'Right.'

'They're impatient, being back inside for the winter.' Her gaze turned to the fields, her voice thick with emotion as she continued. 'Coming back here... Well, I wished it could have been for different reasons. Dad loved this place, and he knew I did too. That's why he left it to me. It wasn't a hard decision to stay.'

'I'm still amazed how you cope with everything,' Kyle admitted, concerned for her, in awe of her strength and determination.

'The place can't pay its own way now. I have to work if I want to keep it. And I do want that. More than anything.'

They returned to the kitchen and Alexandra poured him a mug of coffee.

'Thanks.' He watched her, desperately wanting her back in his arms.

For now she was busy again, putting food bowls in the porch and outside the back door for the cats, who approached cautiously, regarding him with wary suspicion. Next it was Max's turn. But, just as Kyle hoped Alex was done and he could reclaim her attention, she edged towards the door, looking nervous and uncertain.

'I'll, um, just have a shower and get dressed.'

Sipping his coffee, he watched her go, a frown creasing his brow. 'To hell with this,' he muttered after a moment, setting his half-empty mug in the sink and following her.

She was already under the shower spray when he arrived in the bathroom, unaware of his presence as he shed his clothes and left them in a heap on the floor with hers before stepping in behind her. She gasped as he slid his arms around her, drawing her back against him.

'Kyle!'

'It's more environmentally friendly to share. It conserves water and electricity.'

He felt the chuckle ripple through her. 'Is that right?'

'Mmm. Besides, I missed you. Needed you.'

He bent his head, setting his mouth to her shoulder, nipping her soft, golden flesh with his teeth before salving the sting with his tongue, making her moan. Taking the soap, he worked up a lather before slowly and intimately re-learning her body. He lingered over the generous swell of her full, firm breasts, teasing the nipples that peaked enticingly against his palms, then his hands moved down over the smooth curve of her belly, pausing to explore her sensitive navel before sliding downwards again. She whimpered, instinctively widening her stance, and he used one hand to cup between her legs.

'Anatomy was always my favourite subject,' he mouthed against her skin.

'Kyle…'

Smiling, he wrapped his free arm round her waist in support and her hands gripped his forearm as she sagged against him, writhing in his hold, her whole body shaking as his fingers explored, teased and tormented. His mouth tasted her skin, teeth nibbling, tongue caressing, before his lips worked up her neck to her ear where he knew she was so sensitive, licking the hollow before sucking on her lobe, whispering to her about all the naughty things he wanted to do with her. A sob escaped her and he tightened his hold, bracing her against him as his fingers moved more insistently, until she flew over the edge and she cried out her pleasure. He allowed her trembling body to turn, holding her tight as she pressed close, her arms winding round him as their mouths met… open, hot, hungry. Kyle lost himself in the kiss then, impatient and needy, he snapped off the water and reached for a towel, hastily drying them before he swept her up in his arms and carried her back to her room.

He dropped her unceremoniously on the bed before following her down, licking the lingering drops of moisture from her skin, taking his time, his hands exploring while his mouth loved her breasts. Gasping, her fingers burrowed into his hair, holding him to her, her body arching against him. Smiling against her skin, he slowly worked his way to her navel before moving down.

'No!' she whimpered, her body belying her as she moved instinctively to his touch.

'Yes!'

'I can't.'

He chuckled at her feeble protest, loving the way her flesh trembled, and the little sighs and moans she couldn't contain as she responded to him with wild abandon. 'Sure you can. I could do this for hours.'

'Oh... Kyle!'

He was in heaven. Once more he pushed her past the point of no return, loving her sensuality, how reactive she was, how sensitive to his touch. As aftershocks rippled through her he slid back up her body and drew her into his arms, feeling the thud of her heartbeat as it gradually slowed. He cradled her, smiling when she stirred, allowing her to push him over, his breath catching at the sultry look in her smoky grey eyes.

'My turn,' she insisted.

Kyle willingly gave himself up to the indescribable magic of her hands and her mouth enjoying his body. And, when he couldn't stand the exquisite torture another minute, he rolled her back under him.

'Don't wait,' she begged, her voice a husky whisper. 'Now. Please.'

Any thought he had of taking his time vanished at her impassioned demand. He reached out for a condom, his body shaking as she took it from him and rolled it on, caressing him, driving him mad, her eyes darkening with answering need, tempting him beyond bearing as she drew him down to her, wrapping her legs around him. Helpless, he lost himself in her, caught in the magic between them. They clung together, as if needing to stay grounded while the fiery passion flared out of control once more. Overcome by the ecstasy, they finally collapsed together, their breathing laboured, their hearts thudding madly. Kyle eased his weight off her, gathering her close, never wanting to let her go.

'You're amazing, Lexie. It's never been like this before. I've never desired anyone as I do you,' he murmured as she cuddled against him and he admitted to himself that he wanted her here, like this, in his arms, forever.

Alex moved around the kitchen preparing a hurried meal. They had been reluctant to get out of bed, but the time had passed all too swiftly, and Kyle had to get back to Rigtownbrae to fulfil his promise to cover the BASICS shift for Hannah. Alex didn't want him to go, didn't want real life to intrude on the fantasy world they had created these last hours.

Kyle said he'd always enjoyed anatomy. Alex smiled. He was very good at it, and he certainly knew exactly what to do with hers! Nothing had prepared her for the magnitude of sensation, abandonment and sheer joy of making love with Kyle Sinclair. Unleashed, he was the most intensely sensual and physical man she had ever met. His stamina was impressive, too! She stifled a giggle, easing her position, feeling all the delicious aches in her body from the hours of pleasure they had shared together. He was wickedly naughty in the most delicious of ways, and she had responded to him with all inhibitions stripped away. Nothing else in her life was ever going to be like this; she just knew it. What she didn't know was where they went from here, if—

The phone rang, interrupting her reverie, and she moved to answer it.

'Did you enjoy your night with Kyle? It's the only one you're going to get.'

The icy words from an all-too-familiar source tightened her

stomach and dampened the glow she had been feeling just moments before. 'Was there something specific you wanted, Penny?' she asked politely, determined not to be intimidated by the woman, refusing to ask how she had known Kyle was here with her, not wanting to consider that he might have told her.

'If you think you mean anything to him you are foolishly mistaken. You know why he pays you any attention at all, don't you? You know why he shared your bed?' the other woman asked, a sneer in her hard, flat voice.

'I'm sure you plan to enlighten me as to your views.'

If anything, Penny's voice turned harsher, colder. 'You're nothing but a passing fancy, Alex. Kyle's future is with me, he turns to me to meet his needs and he always will do, long after you have gone from Glenside. And, believe me, you will be gone. Soon. He plays this little game because you look like Helen, his ex-wife. He sees you and thinks of her. You're just too stupid to realise that he used you to get her out of his system. Don't expect more than a night. He'll be coming home to me now.'

The connection was broken, but it took a moment before Alex could replace the receiver. Her hand shook and a chill shivered down her spine. She didn't want to listen to Penny, didn't want to believe her, but… Was it true she looked like the woman who had left Kyle and broken his heart? Was that really all he saw when he looked at her? Whatever she thought of Penny and her games, her comments had sown new seeds of doubt and made her feel insecure. She should ask Kyle for answers, but she was too scared, too fragile, too confused after the last hours with him.

However vindictive and maliciously delivered they had been, hadn't Penny's words only confirmed her own fears that Kyle was not ready for any kind of relationship after being betrayed by his ex-wife? Her doubts increased as she recalled the way he had come to her to talk over his lost baby. He wasn't over what had happened to him, and she couldn't be sure at the moment where his emotions really lay. She cared deeply for him but she wasn't cut out for a meaningless fling. Until she was sure of Kyle's intentions, perhaps she should cool things, guard her own heart, give him time.

He came into the kitchen then, dressed and ready to leave, a frown on his face as he looked at her. 'Is something wrong?'

'No.' Hand unsteady, she hung up and moved away from the phone, wrapping her arms protectively around her stomach as she tried a stiff smile, unable to meet his eyes. 'I'm fine.'

She turned away, fussing with the snack she had prepared, her mind reeling. Everything now felt awkward between them, and she didn't know if she could trust her own feelings—or if she could trust Kyle. It wasn't just Penny's revelations. She'd already had doubts before last night, and in their time together they hadn't talked about anything important, had just given in to the incredible physical desire between them. But what did she really know of Kyle's motives, his feelings? She needed to give them space, needed to pretend she was sophisticated and worldly and wasn't making demands on him.

'Alexandra?'

So they were back to that? 'Lexie' had been forgotten? Tense and scared, she set the plates on the table. 'The food's ready. Help yourself.'

'We need to talk.'

'What about?' she managed, clenching her hands in her lap, her nails digging into her palms, fighting for the courage to give him the chance of an easy exit…hoping like hell that he wouldn't take it and confirm she had been right to doubt him.

He sat at the table, not touching his meal, and she could almost feel his confusion across the distance that separated them. A distance that seemed to widen by the minute. 'About this, about us.'

'It's all right, Kyle, I'm not expecting anything from you,' she told him with a false smile, trying to keep her turbulent emotions out of her voice, scared he was going to dismiss what they had or diminish it. She needed to be strong. 'We had a nice time together. We both know it doesn't have to be more than that.'

It didn't *have* to be more but, oh, how she wanted it to be. Desperately. The silence stretched, and she was hurting so much she was sure her heart was going to shatter into a million pieces. She wanted him to argue, to reassure her, to tell her she was wrong, to fight for what they had. But he didn't. Instead, he rose to his feet and moved away from her, leaving her feeling his emotional and physical withdrawl.

'Then there's nothing left to say,' he stated, his voice strained.

Time seemed to stand still. Alex sat there, disbelieving, wanting to call him back, but he turned from her and walked out of the room, closing the back door quietly behind him. She heard his car start, listened to the sound of the tyres crunching on the gravel, then the engine fading as he drove away. Leaving her alone. Lost. Utterly bereft. So, she had her answer. Kyle wasn't over his past. He wasn't ready for a relationship. He didn't want her—not for more than a night or two.

Alex squeezed her eyes closed but tears escaped between her lashes and trickled down her cheeks. What a fool she had been, ignoring her doubts, believing in fairy tales and happy-ever-afters. Being with Kyle had surpassed her wildest dreams. But that's all their time together had been—a dream. Not real. A moment out of time. Kyle had taken her places she had never been to before, she had done things with him she would never do with anyone else as she had trusted him implicitly with her body and her heart. Now her heart felt broken beyond repair.

Kyle had gone and she feared she meant nothing to him at all.

CHAPTER TEN

'KYLE, we have a problem,' Lisa Sharpe announced, closing the consulting-room door and taking a seat by his desk.

Kyle glanced up. He felt like telling Lisa he had a lot of problems. The principal one being Alexandra. Damn it. He didn't want to think of her every second of every day. She'd made her feelings clear enough, there was nothing he could do about it, but he just didn't understand what had happened, how things had changed so drastically so quickly, leaving him scared, confused, angry. *We had a nice time together. We both know it doesn't have to be more than that.* Nice? How could she have reduced the most magical, incredible night of his life to something so meaningless, so unimportant? There was nothing to suggest she hadn't been as fully committed as he had been, that she didn't want more, but clearly he had made another foolish mistake, and had given his trust too soon.

He frowned, thinking back to that horrible scene in her kitchen. He'd heard the telephone ring as he'd finished getting dressed, and had come to the kitchen to see her by the phone, all colour drained from her face. Who had called her? What had they said to upset her? Did that have something to do with the change in her and her decision to send him away? Frightened, he had reacted without thinking, had bitten back confessions about his feelings for her, believing from her casual words that their time together had meant far more to him than it had to her. That it was over between them. Alexandra was backing off, retreating, and he didn't know what to do, how to handle it.

'Kyle, are you listening?'

'Sorry, Lisa.' He shook his head, trying to focus. 'What's happened?'

'I've had Charles Frazer on the phone. His wife, Winnie, is one of your patients. Asthma. She is also one of those who didn't turn up for her last regular appointment when she was meant to see Alex to check her flows and so on.'

Kyle's eyes narrowed. Lisa now had his full attention. 'Go on.'

'Winnie is home and recovering, but she had a nasty attack and had to go to casualty,' Lisa explained, her frown deepening. 'Charles is furious and says someone from the surgery phoned to cancel her last appointment.'

'What? Who would do such a thing?'

'He says it is our negligence that made Winnie so ill.'

Kyle swore under his breath. 'What's going on, Lisa?'

'You know I've been looking into the issue of the missing appointments?'

'Yes. And the mix up with the home visits, too,' he reminded her.

Lisa nodded. 'I can tell you that no more of those have happened, but I believe the computer records were tampered with.'

'Who?'

'Just a minute. Alex raised the problems with me and I've rung several of the people who haven't turned up for their appointments with her.' Lisa paused a moment, shaking her head. 'They all say that they received a phone call telling them they didn't need to come in.'

'And?' he prompted, a sense of foreboding bringing a tight knot to his stomach.

'Each one says that the person who called them gave Alex's name.'

Kyle swore again and rose to his feet, pacing the room, struggling to take it in. All Penny's warnings came back to him—that Alexandra wasn't as she seemed, not to trust her. He sat down and angrily thumped his hand on the desk. 'Tell Alexandra to come and see me, I want to talk to her about this.'

'Don't do that, Kyle. Not now. Please. I know you are angry, so am I, but I honestly don't believe Alex has anything to do with this,' Lisa insisted.

'What makes you so sure?' He wanted to believe, to trust Alexandra, but… 'Have you evidence to the contrary?'

'Not yet, but I think I know where we can get some.'

Kyle sighed, running a hand through his hair. 'I'm listening.'

'Look, it isn't my business, I don't know what is going on between you and Alex, but you've both been tense and miserable this week, avoiding each other the like the plague. All I know is that Alex is the best nurse we've ever had. Everyone loves her, staff and patients alike. The only person here who has anything bad to say about her is Penny.' Lisa paused and Kyle watched her, seeing her uncertainty. 'Penny had it in for Alex from the first, Kyle, and has been awful to her. I've heard things—nothing I have concrete proof on—but my advice from all my experience is to give Alex a chance. She was the one who brought this to our attention in the first place. Why would she do that if she was the one causing the problem?'

It was true, that side of it didn't make any sense. And, yes, if he thought about it clearly, leaving his own personal issues and feelings for Alexandra aside, it was only Penny who had subtly and consistently whispered in his ear to make him doubt. What was going on? He suddenly thought about something he had filed away to investigate but with the events of last Sunday had put out of his mind.

'I still want to speak to Alexandra, hear her side of the story. And I want to speak to some of the patients myself. I'll go round to see Charles and Winnie today.' He rested his arms on his desk. 'Before that, I want you to tell me something, Lisa. Why has Alexandra been working longer hours and more weekend shifts than anyone else?'

Lisa's gaze slid from his. 'You know who does the district nurses' rota.'

'Penny?'

'Yes.'

Silence stretched, and he fidgeted in agitation. 'What's going on, Lisa?'

'I told you, Penny doesn't like Alex, so she gives her the longest journeys and the most difficult patients. And she's been taking advantage, skipping her own weekend duties, claiming to be sick and making sure that Alex has to fill in at the last minute.'

'I see.'

'I doubt it,' the older woman muttered under her breath.

Kyle's frown deepened. 'And what does Penny do?'

'Who knows?' Lisa's laugh had a bitter edge. 'Has her hair done, most likely.'

Jaw tightening, he ignored the sarcasm—for now. 'Why hasn't Alexandra said anything?'

'Who to? Penny isn't going to give her a break, quite the opposite given the snide remarks she's always making about her and her work. And Alex wouldn't—'

'What?' he pressed as the words snapped off.

'Nothing. It doesn't matter.'

'Yes, it does. Lisa, tell me. Please.'

'Alex believes you'd side with Penny.'

'Why would I do that?' he riposted stiffly, his body tense at the accusation.

'Penny has let it be known how close you are with her, and she seems to have done an equally good job of convincing you to doubt Alex.'

The words stung, as did the realisation that people in the practice saw him as being likely to give preferential treatment to Penny. He frowned, thinking back with discomfort over the things Penny had said to him these last weeks, the subtle hints she had dropped about Alexandra. What was Penny doing? And why? Unwanted thoughts raced through his mind. Had Penny done this before? Maybe he'd been so wrapped up in his own troubles that he hadn't seen what was happening, but he'd always imagined Penny was his friend, that she wanted what was best for him, supported him. If she didn't… The thought lingered uncomfortably.

'Could you give me a list of the other patients who received these phone calls? After I've spoken to them, I'll go to the Frazer's. And, Lisa, please ask Alexandra to come and see me when she is free.'

'All right. I'll bring the list shortly.' Lisa rose to her feet and lingered a moment, seemingly reluctant to leave. 'Kyle, please think about what I have said. Don't take this out on Alex, I know she isn't involved.'

'Just send her in, Lisa.'

Although how the hell he could bear to be in the same room with her, look at her, talk with her and pretend nothing had happened, that he didn't ache for her, care for her, he didn't know.

Alex was furious. After her final patient left on Friday morning, she turned her attention to the report she had compiled about Penny, complete with patient testimonies, and added the final piece to it before printing out several copies, one for each of the doctors, one for Lisa and one for herself. Just in case. She no longer trusted the computer system, not now she and Lisa suspected someone had been able to manipulate records on at least one occasion.

Today she had received another report from a tearful patient about Penny's disrespect and poor care. She was still shocked and seething with fury about the elderly woman who had been left naked in a bath for over an hour—cold, frightened and unable to move on her own. Penny had dumped her in the bath, had gone off to run some personal errand or other, and had been despicably rough and rude to the distressed woman when she had finally returned.

It was past time she presented her report to the doctors in charge of the practice. She knew that, had made the decision, but she still felt nervous. If she reported Penny officially or unofficially to Robert or Elizabeth, it would appear as if she was going behind Kyle's back. But if she went to Kyle about the problem, what would he do? He cared about his patients, she knew that, but she was uncertain what place Penny had in his life. While she hated to doubt him, would he put his feelings for the other woman first and protect her?

In truth, she wasn't sure how to read him. Not after this last week. She tried so hard not to think about the way he had left on Sunday after their stupendous night together, tried not to cry again over what had been lost, the way he appeared to have tossed it all back in her face as if it was just a casual one-night stand. And Penny's accusations still haunted her, fuelling her own doubts. Had Kyle only given her any attention because she reminded him of his ex-wife? Had he really just used her for his own ends? Would he ever be ready to move on?

They had done their best to ignore each other at the surgery this week, but every time she caught a glimpse of him or heard his voice it was like another death knell to her shattered heart. He had not given the slightest sign that he wished to speak to her, to discuss what had happened, to remember what had passed between them, so she had done her best to hide her emotions and remain professional at work. But it cost her. Big time. She couldn't sleep, couldn't eat, and she felt as if she was dying inside. But she played by the rules he set, kept her distance from him and tried to remain cool on the occasions they were forced to work together, because she didn't want to make even more of a fool of herself or embarrass anyone or, heaven forbid, break down and beg him for answers. It made for a difficult working relationship and a strained atmosphere around the surgery.

She had stewed over the problem of Penny for some time, unable to find a way out but unable to ignore it. Now things with Kyle had deteriorated to such a degree, she no longer cared about her own position, unsure if she could even go on working in Rigtownbrae, having to see him, work with him and never be able to touch him again. Most importantly of all, she had to do right by the patients who depended on her, who were too scared to speak up for themselves without her help. If she acted as advocate for the patients and lost her job in the process, so be it. Somehow she would manage. If there were no practice or district nurse vacancies at Lochanrig or Glentown-on-Firth, she would try other surgeries, or take a position at the hospital if she had to. It wasn't what she wanted but she needed the work to keep her home. She wasn't going to allow Kyle, Penny or anyone else to take that away from her.

'Are you free?' Lisa asked, coming into the nurses' room.

'Yes, I've finished my appointments for the morning, and all the paperwork is up to date.'

Lisa sat down, concern on her face. 'You're looking tired, Alex, and pale. What's wrong?'

'Nothing,' she lied, fighting back an unwanted sting of tears. 'I'm fine. Any news on the missed appointments?'

'Yes, that's what I came to talk with you about.'

Alex listened in shock as Lisa outlined what she had discovered. 'But I never phoned any of them!' she protested, her stomach churning.

'I know.' The older woman reached out and patted her arm. 'I have every faith in you, Alex, and I have my suspicions about who is doing this. I've said as much to Kyle, but he wants to talk with you.'

'Oh, no!' She couldn't face him, especially if he had doubts about her. The realisation made her even more heartsick. 'He doesn't think I did this, does he?'

Lisa's momentary hesitation was telling, and pain seared through her. 'I'm sure he doesn't, not in his heart of hearts. And we're going to sort this out, Alex, I promise you. Try and be patient with him, lovey, he's been through so much—I think you know that—and it takes him a while to trust again. I think you two are perfect for each other. I can see you are hurting, but if you care about Kyle, hang in there.'

Alex didn't know what to say. The practice manager was not only good at her job, she was very perceptive about the people she worked with, and underneath her efficient, businesslike exterior she had a heart of gold. 'I'll try.' She knew what Kyle had faced, knew it was hard for him, yet he had done little this last week to make her believe they had any kind of future.

'Good girl. Now, have you finished the report on Penny?'

'Yes.' Alex turned and collected the files. 'I have the copies here.'

'Give me one—and copies for Robert and Elizabeth. I'll

explain to them and hand them over later,' Lisa suggested briskly. 'That way you'll have some back-up.'

She was grateful for Lisa's support and wished Kyle felt the same way. 'Thank you.'

'Now, you take the other copy along to Kyle and have your say, don't let all that brooding and pouting put you off. He will come round,' she reassured.

Alex wished she had as much faith. She stood outside his consulting-room door a few moments later, her heart pounding madly, her body shaking in reaction to the thought of seeing him, scared that he wouldn't believe in her, that he would side with Penny, that this would be the real end of any chance they had of sorting things out. She was a grown woman. It was about time she acted like one, put her own emotions aside and protected her patients. She squared her shoulders, drew in a deep breath and knocked on the door.

'Come in.'

The sound of Kyle's voice was enough to send a shiver rippling down her spine. She stepped into the room and her gaze clashed with his. Her breath caught when she saw how tired and unhappy he looked, but his deep blue eyes were cold and expressionless. Clutching the report to her chest as if it could protect her in some way, she stood her ground. 'You wanted to see me?'

'Yes.' He looked down at a piece of paper on his desk and Alex swallowed, fighting down memories of how his wayward dark hair had felt beneath her fingers, how his mouth had tasted when he had kissed her with such wanton passion, of the touch of his hands on her, how his perfect, leanly muscled body had moved so erotically with her own. 'It's about the missed appointments. I'm going to see Charles and Winnie Frazer shortly, but I've called all the people on the list Lisa gave me and every one of them claim that they received a phone call cancelling their check-ups—from you.'

'I see. And you believe that of me?' she asked, bitter disappointment lancing inside her. Even though she had been prepared for this, it hurt more than she could imagine possible.

'I didn't say that.' He sighed, running the fingers of one hand through his hair, dislodging a couple of locks which fell across his forehead. Alex closed her eyes. 'I want to hear your side of things, Alexandra.'

'I never called any of those people.'

'Then how do you explain it?' he demanded, voice flat, giving her no indication of his mood.

Determined to maintain control, she forced herself to meet his gaze. 'I can only assume someone else made those calls and pretended to be me.'

'Really.' A frown creased his brow, his eyes watchful as he leaned back in his chair and regarded her like some specimen under a microscope. 'And who would do something like that?'

'I can think of one person...but I doubt you'll like it.'

'Try me.'

Alex clutched the file more closely to her. 'It isn't any secret that Penny has been trying to undermine me ever since I arrived here. She seems to have succeeded as far as you're concerned. She has told me to my face she will do all she can to make me leave, but what I didn't expect was her to put patients' lives at risk to do it.'

'That's a serious accusation,' Kyle warned her but she was too angry to care.

'So is the one you are making against me.' She sucked in a breath, trying to control her tone, to ignore how much this was hurting her. 'I have received a number of testimonies from patients about Penny's lack of care, starting with the incident my first week here with Bill Campbell's catheter and pressure sore. They have all been too scared to speak up, but have given me permission to do so on their behalf. You'll find all the information in here,' she continued, setting the file on his desk. 'Lisa knows about it, she has copies for Robert and Elizabeth. Sack me if you want to, I'm not bothered about me. All tha matters is the care of the patients. And I really don't think I can work here any longer anyway.'

'Alexandra—'

She cut off his shocked exclamation, needing to get th words out while she still could. 'I trusted you in the mos ultimate way possible—with my body, in my bed. But it's no enough for you, is it? I'm not her…your ex-wife. And I'm no Penny. I've tried not to listen to all the things she's told me these last weeks, but her phone call on Sunday was the fina straw and really just confirmed all the doubts I already ha that you're not over the past.' Her voice cracked and she bi her lip, willing herself not to cry.

'What are you talking about?' He rose to his feet, and she backed away as he rounded the desk towards her. 'What has Penny said?'

'Ask her yourself. I can't do this any more, Kyle, I just can't.'

'Lexie…'

Tears spilled down her cheeks at his hoarse plea. 'Leave me alone. Please.'

She pushed past him and ran from the room. It was finished, over. She'd given him the truth about Penny. Wha he did with it was up to him. Despite Lisa's reassurances, she felt there was really no way back from here. She'd lost Kyle He didn't believe in her. All she could do was find another jo and move on.

What the hell was going on? By the time Kyle had gathere his scattered wits, Alexandra had left the building. He curse with frustration. Had it really been Penny on the phone o Sunday morning? Although he had sensed moments whe

Alexandra had been distancing herself, that call was the moment when things had changed irrevocably between them but he had been too shocked, too hurt, to question her at the time. What had Penny told her? Whatever it was had increased Alexandra's doubts and made her back off.

He dragged his fingers through his hair in agitation. Rather than withdrawing into himself for protection, he should have trusted Alexandra, should have known she was different, should have demanded to know what was wrong. Instead of fighting for them and what they had, he'd let her down, let himself down. Not any more. He had a lot to do if he hoped to get Alexandra back. Filled with determination, his thoughts as dark as his expression, he went in search of Lisa to put things in motion.

First stop was the Frazers.

'I wanted to come round myself to say how very sorry we are about what happened. It is being investigated now, and I promise you we will get to the bottom of it,' Kyle assured them as he sat in the cosy living room and addressed Charles and Winnie Frazer.

'We appreciate that, Dr Sinclair,' Charles allowed, reaching out for his wife's frail hand. 'It fair shook Win up, I can tell you.'

'It must have been a horrible experience for both of you. Can you tell me exactly what happened when you received the phone call?'

Winnie nodded. 'I was home on my own. Charles had gone to the shops before taking me to the surgery. But the phone rang and the woman said she was Nurse Alex Patterson, and there had been a revision of my file and I didn't have to come in so regularly for checks,' she explained, her pale face a study of concentration as she recalled the event.

'We were very surprised, given how unstable Win's asthma has been,' Charles added.

'I understand.' Kyle smiled, nerves twisting inside him as he asked the next question. 'And it was definitely Nurse Patterson?'

'Yes,' Winnie admitted, and his heart sank.

'That's certainly what the caller said. Win wanted me to hear the news so she left the answer-machine recording on,' Charles explained.

Kyle's gut tightened. 'Have you wiped the tape? Might the message still be on it?'

'I'm sure it is,' Charles responded, rising to his feet. 'Would you like to listen to it?'

'If I may. Thank you.'

Kyle waited with edgy impatience as Charles fiddled with the machine and trawled through a couple of irrelevant messages until he found the right one. Then the voice came across loud and clear, and he felt sick to his stomach because there was now no doubt at all. He knew who had been phoning patients and cancelling appointments. And he had proof.

'That's it.' Charles switched off the machine.

'Would it be all right if I borrowed the tape? I can make sure it is returned to you, but I'd like it as evidence so we can clear this matter up at the surgery once and for all.'

Winnie smiled, seemingly delighted to be caught up in some excitement. 'It all sounds very cloak and dagger, doesn't it, Charles?'

If it wasn't so serious, Kyle might have shared their amusement. But he felt betrayed, cheated. He'd been lied to. And now he had to see his partners and arrange for them to take the most serious action possible. Anger and confusion raged inside him as he made his way back to Glenside and made the necessary preparations.

He was feeling tense when Penny entered the meeting room. She looked sleek, polished and supremely confident, the pale blue eyes reflecting a cool, cunning gleam, making him wonder why he had never noticed her sly side before. She had been supportive through his divorce and he had considered her a friend, of sorts, certainly a respected colleague. But again he had been proved wrong, had given his trust unwisely. He hadn't wanted to believe the evidence in the file Alexandra had provided, but the information had checked out in every respect. He felt duped, furiously angry at what their patients had suffered in silence, filled with disgust that any nurse could abuse and disrespect someone in their care. Robert and Elizabeth were in full agreement about what had to be done.

'What is this all about, Kyle? I have plans for the evening.' She tossed her thick red braid over her shoulder and fixed her gaze on him, her smile obvious. 'Of course, I could cancel them for you…if you're ready. Now you've scratched the itch with dull, homely Alex and she doesn't want you, that is.'

'This isn't about Alexandra, Penny. And it isn't about me. It's about you and a file full of evidence of your abuse of patients,' he stated, unable to keep the harshness and disgust from his voice.

Shards of ice appeared in the blue eyes. 'Oh, please. Has little Miss Goody-Two-Shoes been telling tales out of turn again? She has you wrapped round her little finger, doesn't she, Kyle?'

'I told you, this is about you. Why, Penny?' he demanded. 'Why the lack of care for patients?'

'I have a busy schedule, I don't have time for the whingers and those who cling and demand too much. Many of them could help themselves if they put their mind to it, many are ill because of their own actions. No one can be there all the time or give them everything.'

Kyle shook his head in disbelief. He didn't know this callous woman at all. 'Why on earth would you choose to be a nurse with an attitude like that? All our patients deserve respect and dignity and the best care we can give. Clearly you can't provide any of that.'

Folding her arms, expression blank, Penny refused to answer.

'Why did you try to set Alexandra up for a fall, tampering with patient lists and cancelling appointments? Don't try to deny it,' he warned as she made to interrupt. 'We have you on tape impersonating Alexandra when you called patients. Do you want to hear it?'

'Clearly there's no point in denying it,' she stated with an air of defiance that grated on his nerves and raised his temper to new levels.

'So why? What has Alexandra ever done to you?'

Penny's smile was pitying. 'She's pulling the wool over your eyes, Kyle, making a fool of you.'

'No, Penny, it is you who have been making a fool of everyone. It stops now. You're finished here.'

'You can't do this to me,' she shouted, pretence stripped away. 'Why do you think I've been hanging round this dump for two years?'

Kyle sighed, suddenly tired of the whole charade. 'I've no idea.'

'Waiting for you.'

'What?'

'I've been solving your problems, making them go away, waiting for you to stop wallowing and start living again. I want you, I deserve you, I've worked for you. Do you think I was going to stand by and let some other woman waltz in here and take you away from me?'

'What are you talking about?' Shocked, angry, he stared at her in bemusement. 'What do you mean, you deserve me, made my problems go away?'

'God, you are so stupid. I made your timid, frigid little wife go away for you, didn't I? Made sure you were free of her. She wasn't right for you. Neither is Alex. Now it's time for us. We'll be good together. We can go away from here, start a new life.'

'You're insane. There has never been anything between us and there never will be.' He felt sick, disgust welling inside him. 'You have no idea about me, or my life or my feelings. None of which include you. In any capacity. Not then, not now, not ever.'

'Well, don't think Alex will want you. Not now. I've seen to that,' she taunted.

Temper threatened to get the better of him. 'How did you know I had stayed with Alexandra? What did you say to her on the phone?'

'I knew you were going to the dinner. I watched your house. When you didn't come home, I drove by and saw your car at Alex's place,' she informed him as if it was a normal thing to do. 'As for what I said, I just told her a few home truths. Come on, Kyle, what other woman but me would put up with your sulky moods and this ridiculous grief you hang on to over what was little more than some malformed foetus?'

'Get out.' The order came out icy-calm, although fury raged within him. He rose to his feet, his eyes narrowed to slits as he faced down the woman he had looked on in dark days as a friend but who had betrayed and manipulated him. 'Your severance pay will be sent on, but don't expect any kind of reference. You're not welcome here any more.'

'Kyle—'

'Get out of my sight.'

'You can't do this,' she spat. 'I'll talk to Robert and Elizabeth, I'll—'

'We already know, Penny,' Robert stated, stepping forward with Elizabeth from where they had been waiting out of sight.

'We know everything, we heard it all. You are finished here, finished in nursing. We'll see to that. You will not contact any one of our staff or patients—should you try to, we'll take legal action. Leave now or I shall have you removed. You'll be hearing from the nursing authorities in due course.'

As if realising she had played her final card and lost, Penny glared at them one last time. 'Damn you all to hell,' she cursed, before spinning away and slamming the door behind her.

Kyle slumped to his chair, feeling as if the solid ground he had been standing on for the last eighteen months had been ripped out from beneath him, leaving him rootless. He couldn't sort out all the jumbled emotions and facts in his head.

'I'm sorry, Kyle.' Robert's words were sad and full of concern. 'You did what you had to do.'

'We are all behind you. And we were all taken in by her, so don't blame yourself,' Elizabeth added.

Not everyone had been taken in, had they? Not Lisa. Not Alexandra. Lexie... He groaned, all at sea over her, so unsure of her feelings for him. If she even had any now. What had Penny done? What had she said to drive Alexandra away? More importantly, could he ever hope to win her back? He knew he had to try all in his power to make it happen. But he also had other things he needed to do, to understand, to sort out, before he could go to her. Penny had given him advice, and had given Helen advice all those months ago. He had been so wrapped up in his grief, his hurt, that he had taken Penny's friendship at face value. Now he knew he had been wrong. How much else had he been wrong about back then? What had really happened? What had Penny told Helen? How had Penny conspired to drive the wedge deeper between himself and Helen and their already rocky marriage?

If Penny had really cared a jot for him, she would not have done so much to hurt him. That he had allowed her to even go so far as neglecting patients made him sick to his stomach. He didn't care about himself but he did care about his patients and staff…and about Alexandra.

Now he had to put things right. He just hoped it wasn't too late. But he had to face the past before he could hope to offer Alexandra a future.

He looked at his partners, knew they would support him. 'I need to go away for a couple of days.'

'Whatever you have to do, Kyle,' Robert stated, and Elizabeth nodded her agreement.

'I'll be in touch.'

Rising to his feet, he prepared to put his fledgling plans into action. First he had a couple of phone calls to make, things to arrange, before taking a trip to Ayrshire. Then, hopefully, he could come back to Rigtownbrae and claim Alexandra for his own.

CHAPTER ELEVEN

IT HAD been the strangest weekend. Alex had tried to keep busy—and goodness knew, there'd been enough chores awaiting her attention—but she had felt listless, heartsick, troubled about what was going to happen at work and with Kyle.

Part of her had wanted him to phone or visit but as Friday night became Saturday, and Saturday became Sunday, she had given up hope of any word from him or any reconciliation. At least she still had a job…for now. Lisa had rung to tell her to come in on Monday as usual, that she would be out in the community doing home visits. Which was a relief. It meant she wouldn't have to see Kyle. But Lisa had said nothing else, had given no word about Penny, and Alex was left worried, her imagination running riot.

She had pretty much made up her mind that she would have to leave Glenside and find work elsewhere when the phone had rung on Saturday evening and Conor's reassuring voice had greeted her.

'You sound low, sweetie. Is everything all right?' he asked.

'Not really.' She had to bite back a sudden threat of tears, knew Conor had heard it in her voice. 'Things aren't going to work out at Rigtownbrae.'

'Would you like me or Kate to come over for a chat?'

She was grateful for the offer—they were wonderful people and she was so fond of them—but she couldn't forget they were Kyle's friends and she didn't want to make the situation more difficult. 'No, I'll be fine.'

'Ring any time if you change your mind,' Conor insisted. 'We care about both of you, Alex. Don't throw in the towel yet.'

On Sunday afternoon, she was still puzzling over Conor's unexpected phone call and his advice when a car arrived in the driveway. Gravel crunched under tyres and for one heart-stopping moment she thought it might be Kyle. She ran to the kitchen window, her spirits sinking when she realised her visitor was Hannah. Not that she wasn't pleased to see her friend, but…

'Hi,' Hannah greeted her, giving her a hug before she hung up her BASICS jacket in the porch. 'I've been out on a call and thought I'd stop in on the way home and see you.'

'I've just put the kettle on.'

'Great!'

Hannah sat down at the kitchen table and made a big fuss of Max. Frowning, Alex busied herself preparing two mugs of tea. 'I didn't think you were on BASICS duty this weekend.'

'I wasn't, but I took Kyle's shift as he had to go away for a couple of days,' Hannah explained, surprising her.

'Oh.' She didn't want to wonder where he had gone, still less who he had gone with. Penny? The thought cut deep and added to the unbearable hurt weighing her down. 'I see.'

Hannah accepted her mug with a smile of thanks, sympathy and understanding in her gold-flecked eyes. 'Things not going so well?'

'Not really. Work is grim. Things have been happening, making me look bad, but Lisa Sharpe is on my side and knows it wasn't me, that I was set up,' she explained, struggling to mask her feelings of hurt betrayal. 'I presented my report on

Penny. You were right, there were other incidents of her lack of care. But I've not heard back from the doctors what, if anything, they are going to do about it.'

'And Kyle?'

Alex ducked her head, evading Hannah's gaze. 'What about him?'

'We had high hopes for you two,' she confided. 'You're good for each other.'

'It's not going to happen, Hannah. That all got stuffed up, too. I think we both realise where we stand after this last week.'

'But—'

'In fact, I've decided to look for another job,' Alex pressed on, not wanting to talk about Kyle any more. It hurt too much.

Cupping her mug in her hands, Hannah frowned. 'I don't think you should make any hasty decisions, Alex. Sometimes things aren't as bleak as they seem.'

After Hannah left, Alex thought how odd it was that both of Kyle's friends had checked up on her over the weekend. Neither had done that before. Was something going on she didn't know about, or was she just so confused and upset that she was reading more into a perfectly innocent coincidence? She had no answers to any of her questions, just an increasing anxiety about what she would face when she went to work the next morning.

Nervous and edgy, Kyle stood on the doorstep and tried to pluck up the courage to ring the doorbell. He'd spent Saturday with his parents and brother at the farm, talking things through, and now he was here on Sunday afternoon, facing the past, knowing he had to follow through, however difficult it was for them all. Thinking of Alexandra made him both fearful and hopeful, but gave him strength to take the next step. Sucking in a deep breath, he reached out and announced his presence.

The door opened and a gentle hazel gaze widened in shocked surprise. 'Kyle!'

'Hello, Helen.'

'What do you want?' she asked, her voice hardening.

'Can we talk?' he asked, seeing the doubt in her eyes. 'Please. It's very important.'

She hesitated, glancing behind her into the house. 'All right. You'd better come in. Colin is here,' she added, as if in warning.

'That's fine. I'm not here to make any trouble, I just need to ask you something.'

Helen led him through the small, attractive cottage to a traditional kitchen where he had an uneasy meeting with Colin Maxwell. While Helen made tea, Kyle admired the sleeping twins, surprised to find the bitter pain had mellowed and, whilst he was envious, the resentment had vanished. Seeing Helen and Colin again was not proving as difficult as he had feared. He regretted the past, the hurt, the things that had gone wrong—most of all their lost child—but he realised now that he had let go. He didn't love Helen, didn't hate her, just wished her well for her future and hoped he could make a success of his own life from now on.

'I know things were difficult in the past, I'm sorry about that,' he began once they sat down with their tea. 'I hope we can now speak without acrimony and bad feeling.'

'What is it, Kyle? Why have you come?' Helen queried in puzzlement.

He set his cup in the saucer and frowned. 'I need to know what went on back then. Did Penny say things to you?'

'Kyle—'

'Look, I'm not being difficult, I really need to know. It's happening again, Helen, and I don't want to make the same mistakes.' He drew in a deep breath and continued. 'Penny kept telling me you didn't want children, that you were seeing someone else. She said you blamed me when you lost our baby, but you were glad because it meant you didn't have to stay with me, that the best thing was to let you go. Nothing blatant, just little hints and whispers, all insidious and crafty, as she sowed seeds of doubt in my mind at a time when our marriage was already in trouble. It's no excuse but I was under a lot of pressure, grieving for our baby, as you know, and I allowed her to convince me.'

Helen's eyes widened with hurt surprise. 'But that's exactly what she told me! About you. Little asides that you felt I'd trapped you into marriage, that you were secretly glad when I lost our baby, that you never wanted children or me, that you and Penny had something going together. She said that you would be glad if I left you so you could go on with your own life, and she encouraged me to turn to Colin!' she exclaimed, taking her new husband's hand. 'I didn't see any of it clearly, Kyle, not at the time. Now you have confirmed niggling doubts,' she finished with a deep sigh.

'Penny has never been more to me than a colleague and, I wrongly thought, a friend. I was never unfaithful to you,' he assured her now, anger burning inside him. 'So all the time Penny was playing us off against each other, taking advantage of the problems we were having and the breach growing between us? I was so hurt and angry when you married Colin and had the twins with him. I just couldn't come to terms with having lost our baby.' Shaking his head, trying to get his thoughts straight, he ran the fingers of one hand through his hair. 'I'm really sorry, Helen. And I genuinely am pleased that you and Colin are so happy now. I wish you all the best, both of you, and your children. You deserve it.'

Helen's eyes filled with tears. 'Thanks, Kyle. That means a lot to us.' She gave a tremulous smile when Colin confirmed the sentiment. 'I think we both know, though, looking back, that our own marriage wasn't going anywhere, even without Penny's interference,' she added softly.

'You're right. It wasn't just Penny. She was merely the catalyst, spotting what was already broken beyond repair and using that knowledge to her own advantage, for her own sick ends.'

'I know I was wrong, Kyle, to hold you to the marriage in the first place. We cared about each other, I never doubted that, and I always felt so safe with you. But we were more friends than lovers,' Helen admitted, voicing what he had often thought himself over these last painful months.

'Even without Penny, the relationship had been floundering…for both of us. In the end friendship wasn't enough to hold together a marriage that would never have worked.' He paused, collecting his thoughts, shaking his head. 'I know now that having children wouldn't have kept us together, not long term.'

'No, it wouldn't. But I regret losing him, Kyle. Our baby. I always will. Whatever happened to us.'

He nodded in agreement, emotion burning inside him at the thought of his lost son, and the terrible words Penny had flung at him on Friday. 'I still can't believe what Penny did.'

'How did you find out?'

Kyle sighed and explained how Penny's abuse of patients had been unmasked and how, in her anger, she had taunted him with what she had done. 'I had no idea she had those kinds of feelings for me, no clue that she was neglecting patients and continuing her whispering campaign to me and others.'

'She's a manipulator—cold, calculating, clever. It wasn't just you she fooled, Kyle.' Helen paused and regarded him curiously. 'Does this mean there is someone new in your life now?'

'Yes. But I'm not sure she feels the same after whatever Penny has said to her. I hope I can rescue things now I know the truth,' he confessed, closing his eyes as he thought of Alexandra and how important she was to him, his life, his happiness.

'Don't let Penny mess things up again.'

Kyle nodded as he rose to his feet. 'I'm sorry I was so blind before, and both of us had to get hurt and go through what we did.'

'We were both blind. I'm sorry that I wasn't there for you and had no idea what the loss of the baby really meant to you. It was never your fault, Kyle, no one was to blame. We weren't right together, but I hope you will make a go of things with your lady and be happy now.' Helen and Colin saw him out and shook his hand, a new understanding between them. 'Thank you for coming, for setting things straight. Good luck, Kyle.'

'Thanks. You too.'

He left Ayrshire with the answers he needed, but still angry that Penny's calculating lies and scheming had contributed to the wrecking of his already damaged marriage, adding unnecessary pain and ill-feeling. It was true that he and Helen had not shared true love. Had they done, had their marriage been right all along, they would have fought harder to sort things out, would not have given up so easily when things had been hard. But now Penny's actions threatened to destroy what he had with Alexandra, and this time he was fighting tooth and nail for what he wanted…the woman he loved more than anything and needed as much as his next breath. If it wasn't too late. His stomach clenched. All he could think of was how to persuade her to give them another chance.

Alex was just settling her last patient back into bed late on Monday afternoon when her mobile phone bleeped with an incoming message. She glanced at the display, frowning when she noted the urgent appeal for her to call the surgery when she was free. Tension coiled inside her. Was this about Penny?

She'd heard nothing about her report on the other nurse, had heard nothing about Kyle, had no idea if she herself was to be sacked. Casting her worries to the back of her mind, she focused on making her patient—a middle-aged man convalescing after returning home following a serious operation—as comfortable as possible.

'Is there anything else you need before I go, Douglas?' she asked, her smile natural as she fussed with the bed clothes.

'No, lass, you've been wonderful, thank you.' Pale and drawn, he rested back against the pillows. 'My daughter will be in shortly with something to eat.'

Alex lingered, making sure his water, phone and reading materials were within reach. 'You relax, now. Your system's been through a major upheaval, but you're doing well and will be up and about again before you know it.'

'Can't be a day too soon for me.'

'Ring any time if there is anything we can do for you.'

She took her leave, stowed her things in the car, and then sat behind the wheel staring at the brooding outline of the hills in the distance silhouetted against the darkened sky. Sighing, nerves fluttering inside her, she pulled out her mobile phone and rang the surgery.

'Alex, good,' Lisa greeted her briskly. 'I'm sorry, but we've had another call and it is important to fit it in today. No one else is available.'

'All right. I've just finished my last scheduled visit so I can go there now. Can you give me the details?' she asked, resigned to another late night.

'Thanks, lovey.' There was a pause and she could hear Lisa rustling papers. 'The address is here in Rigtownbrae,' she informed her and Alex scribbled it down in her notebook. 'A Mr Smith.'

'What's his situation?'

Another pause followed, and Alex frowned at the reserve in Lisa's voice when the practice manager spoke again. 'He has heart problems. Get there as soon as you can. And let yourself in. I have to go, I have another call on hold,' she finished, hanging up before Alex had the chance to ask more questions.

Pushing her tiredness and inner turmoil aside, Alex drove back to town and found the correct address, not far from the surgery, without any problems. Collecting her bag, unsure what was needed, she walked up the paved pathway and rang the bell to announce her presence before opening the door and stepping inside. The house looked tidy but impersonal, decorated in plain, muted colours with polished wood floors.

'Hello,' she called. 'It's Alexandra Patterson, the district nurse.'

Frowning at the silence, she moved further down the hallway, reviewing the brief but unsatisfactory details she had been given about her patient, concerned for his well-being.

'Mr Smith? Can you hear me? Are you all right?'

Hearing a lock click behind her, she turned round, an involuntary gasp of shock escaping when she saw Kyle leaning back against the front door watching her. Dressed in black jeans and a black jumper, a day's growth of stubble darkening his jaw, he looked dangerous and determined but mind-numbingly gorgeous.

'Hello, Alexandra.'

Her heart started thudding madly under her ribs. 'H-have you been called out too?' She cursed her immediate reaction to him and the telltale breathlessness in her voice, backing away as Kyle began closing the gap between them.

'No.'

'Where's Mr Smith?'

'There is no Mr Smith,' he informed her, that deep, husky voice sending a shiver along her spine.

'Pardon? I don't understand.'

'This is my house.' Her eyes widened in shock, and she continued to retreat as Kyle kept walking. 'I needed to see you and I wasn't sure you would come if you knew it was me.'

The breath lodged in her throat, panic welling inside her. 'Kyle…'

She found herself in a small sitting room, and she tried to manoeuvre round the furniture as he bore down on her. 'Sit down, Lexie.'

'I don't think that's a good idea.' She eyed the door longingly, but he moved to block her escape route. 'I should go now.'

'Not just yet. We need to talk.'

He looked and sounded so serious that she started to fear he had brought her somewhere private to sack her. 'What about?' she murmured, clutching her bag protectively against her, nothing but the width of the settee separating them.

'Everything. Penny. Us.' An intent blue gaze watched her. 'I'm sorry if it seemed that I didn't back you or believe in you.'

It had been more than *seemed* from her perspective. She looked back at him, uncertain, full of hurt and indecision, still unsure where this was going, what it was he wanted. Hard as it was, she tried not to focus on the 'us', knowing they were now past that. Kyle would never be hers.

'Lexie?'

His gruff call reclaimed her attention and she nervously licked her lips. 'What?'

'Will you stay and listen?' His uncharacteristic nervousness affected her more than she could say. 'Please?'

'All right.'

She sighed, giving herself a mental shake, unsure why she could never say no to this man. Relief passed his expression, softening the tension in his face, but he still didn't smile. Instead, he rounded the settee to relieve her of her bag, took her hand in his free one and led her, unprotesting, through to the kitchen where she sat in silence, watching him anxiously.

'Would you like something to drink?' he asked, appearing as nervous as she was. 'Tea, smoothie…or I could open some wine?'

'A smoothie would be nice.'

Nodding, he took two glasses from a cupboard and then crossed to the fridge, pouring the fruity drink from a carton. Alex took the glass he gave her, glad to have something to do with her hands, enjoying the tangy mango and passion-fruit flavour as she sipped the drink.

'I have a lot to tell you.' He sat near her and dragged a hand through his hair. 'Work first. Your report was excellent, invaluable, and we're all really grateful for your courage in taking up the issue for the patients,' he began, and she gazed at him, shocked and delighted. 'I also found out that you and Lisa were right—Penny was behind the campaign to discredit you. Robert, Elizabeth and I were able to confront her late on Friday—you'll be pleased to know she was dismissed with immediate effect. Penny's gone, Lexie. And we'll be reporting her to the nursing authorities, too. She'll be finished as a nurse.'

'Right. Good. I mean, I'm sorry, but…' Her words trailed off as she met his compelling blue gaze.

'Don't be sorry. The patients come first. Always. There is no excuse for anything Penny did.'

Nodding, relieved, she focused on her drink. How did Kyle feel about it all? If Penny had been important to him, this had to be upsetting.

'That's not all, though,' Kyle continued. Her breath caught as she listened to him explain what Penny had done, how she had schemed and lied and betrayed him, coming between him and Helen, helping to drive their troubled marriage further towards the divorce. 'Penny said some terrible things. I had no idea she had planned it all. And she admitted she had done the same with you, telling me lies about you and you lies about me, with the intention of destroying our trust in each other and driving you away. I'm sorry, Alexandra.'

She shook her head, trying to grasp everything he had told her. 'It wasn't your fault, you weren't to know.'

'I should have trusted my feelings for you, trusted the special connection between us. But that Sunday morning I had no idea what was going on. I shouldn't have left, Lexie, but I was confused and angry when you implied what we shared together meant nothing to you,' he admitted frankly.

'I thought you were going to give me the brush off and I couldn't bear hearing you say it, so I said it first, giving you a way out, hoping you wouldn't take it, but thinking it would make it easier for you if you did.'

'Easier?' He stared at her, incredulous. 'It nearly killed me.'

Alex swallowed. 'I was scared.'

'How do you think I felt? For the first time since Helen—even before that—I felt good, had actually opened up, trusted someone with myself.'

'I'm sorry. I thought—'

'What?'

'I already had doubts about whether you were ready for any kind of relationship after all you had been through. And then Penny said it was what you did—casual sex, flings,' she whispered, seeing him blanche, his eyes darkening with a mix of anger and hurt. She almost lost the nerve to carry on but drew in a deep breath, knowing they had to clear the air. 'I—I heard that was how things were and that I… That you thought…' She closed her eyes, unable to face the fierceness in his midnight blue ones. 'It was Penny who rang that day, before you left. I don't know how she knew you were there—'

'She admitted that saw my car wasn't home and drove out to your house,' Kyle told her tiredly, filling in the missing pieces.

Her eyes widened as she considered the lengths Penny had gone to, virtually stalking Kyle. 'Oh!'

'What did Penny say that morning, Alexandra?' he demanded, refocusing her attention.

'She told me that you were together, a couple, that you were using me and only wanted me because I looked like your ex-wife. That you stayed the night not because you cared for me but because you wanted to get Helen out of your system before going back to Penny.'

If anything Kyle looked even more furious, venom in his voice as he swore succinctly. Her alarm increased as he rose to his feet, took her arm and all but towed her with him out of the room. For one frightening moment, she thought he was going to throw her out on the street, but he turned up the stairs instead. She really didn't think it was a good idea to go up there with him, but resistance proved futile, his hold uncompromising as he led her into a bland bedroom. He released her, unspeaking, as he rummaged through some storage boxes in a cupboard and then tossed her a photograph. A wedding photograph. A smiling Kyle, free of the shadows that now darkened his face and clouded his eyes. Alex's eyes widened as she looked at his bride…petite, brunette and nothing remotely like her.

'But Penny said—'

'Penny said a lot of things.' Sighing, he sat down on the end of the bed, looking weary and deflated. 'I went to see them this weekend. Helen and Colin.'

He'd seen his ex-wife? She bit her lip. Did he still love her? 'What happened?' she managed.

'I needed to know the truth. Now I do. I think Helen and I found closure yesterday, and for the first time in a long while

I can put it behind me and move on.' He took her hand and drew her down beside him, explaining how he had cared for Helen but hadn't been in love with her, how tepid their love life had been. 'We both admitted we married for the wrong reasons, friendship was never enough to sustain it, and having a child wouldn't have cemented what was already breaking. If we had truly loved each other then what happened would have brought us closer together, not torn us apart. It wouldn't have been so easy for outside influences to come between us. Penny clearly saw that and played on it to maximise the problems for her own reasons. I was never unfaithful to Helen, and there has been no one since her…until you. Certainly not Penny. That never would have happened.'

Alex swallowed, still stuck on one piece of the information he had given her. 'You hadn't… There was no one at all since Helen?'

'No one but you.'

'Kyle…'

He turned her to face him, his fingers caressing her throat, her neck, making her whole body tremble in response. 'From the moment I saw you I never stood a chance. You messed with my head, got under my skin, stole my heart. I've never been so happy, content, complete as when I'm with you. Our night together was the most magical I've ever known. And thanks to you I've been able to come to terms with what happened, to accept the loss of the baby was a fate of nature and not my fault. For the first time I've been able to believe that life is worth living, that I have a future—if you are part of it.'

There was no doubting his sincerity, and tears stung her eyes as he drew her into his arms. 'Oh, Kyle.'

'Lexie, what we have is too special, too strong, for Penny to have ever permanently come between us or kept us apart.' He cupped her face, his eyes reflecting his every emotion as he looked at her. 'It's true, I do find it hard to trust. I was doubtful if I could ever have a relationship again, and Penny played on those insecurities, but she couldn't stop it, couldn't stop me loving you. And I do love you. So much.'

The tears that had threatened shimmered on her lashes. 'I love you too!'

'I hoped.' A smile both tender and sexy curved his mouth, the pad of one thumb brushing away a bead of moisture that trickled beneath one eye. 'I wasn't sure how you felt. You'd so recently lost your father, you were vulnerable…'

'You're right. We both had issues from the past that made us more cautious, more insecure, and Penny's interference magnified those, played on the doubts already bubbling. I've only had one really serious relationship and that ended on a sour note when Dad was taken ill. Mitchell turned out to be someone I never knew at all. I felt betrayed, foolish. There's been no one since him; I gave all I had to caring for Dad. Then when I met you I was uncertain, not only because of your own reservations but because I had trust issues of my own, both in terms of trusting a man again and in trusting my own judgement.'

Kyle drew her closer and she yearned for his warmth, his touch. 'What I told you that night is true, Lexie. I've never in my life felt the way I do when I'm with you.'

'Nor have I.'

She met his kiss willingly, giving herself up to the moment, tasting him again, seeking his touch, breathing in his scent as she was swept away on the tide of passion that overwhelmed them. Shaking, urgent hands hurried to shed clothes. Mouths met, fingers caressed, stoking the unquenchable flames of desire to a fever pitch, and they fell back on the bed, need consuming them, their coming together frantic, desperate, indescribable.

Later, lying twined in the aftermath of their explosive, earth-shattering union, wondering if their hearts would ever beat normally again, if their breathing would ever slow, Alex forced her eyes open, scared this would turn out to be a dream and not real at all. The first thing she saw was Kyle watching her through eyes turned a dark navy with passion. His sexy smile did dangerous things to her insides. She sucked in a shaky breath and smiled back.

'Hi,' he murmured huskily, the fingers of one hand tracing her jaw, her eyebrows, the outline of her kiss-swollen mouth.

'Hi.' She swallowed at the emotions he made no effort to hide—love, desire, devotion. 'Kyle, I'm sorry for doubting you.'

He shook his head, resting a finger over her lips. 'Don't, sweetheart. Let it go now. We've been over this, our insecurities and doubts made worse because we were both being played by a very calculating woman. It's in the past. We start again from here. OK?'

'OK,' she murmured, distracted as his fingers whispered down towards her breasts.

'In future we talk to each other, discuss our fears and our hopes and our dreams.'

She nodded her agreement, aroused by his touch. 'Always. Can I ask you something?'

'Of course.'

'I know it's silly, but— Why do you never call me "Alex", always "Alexandra"?'

A laugh rumbled from his chest. 'Now I'm going to sound silly!'

She wriggled in his arms, snuggling closer. 'Tell me.'

'Everyone calls you Alex. I don't dislike it, but it's kind of…unisex…and you are most definitely all woman. Alexandra is classy and feminine and special. Like you,' he murmured, his mouth grazing down her throat, his stubble an exciting caress against her skin. 'As for Lexie, that's my private name for the woman I love.'

'Kyle…' Fresh tears, joyful tears, pricked her eyes as she wrapped her arms tightly around him.

'I want to be with you for ever, to marry you, live with you, help you run your place, work with you, grow old with you. I want you to stay nursing at Glenside if that's what you'd like, working alongside me.' He drew back a few inches, eyes heated with desire as laid the palm of one hand on the gentle swell of her belly. 'And I want to watch you bloom with our babies.'

'You want children?'

'Of course.' A frown of concern creased his brow. 'Don't you?'

'Very much. If they're yours. But I thought, after all you had been through, maybe—'

A soft kiss on her lips silenced her. 'I'll never forget, but that is past. What we have is unique, Lexie, the present and the future are ours—for always,' he vowed, and she didn't know how to contain her happiness.

'So how many babies were you thinking of?' she asked with a teasing smile, hugging him close, breathing in the earthy maleness of him, running her hands over the delicious texture of warm, supple skin over taut muscle.

Amusement and desire shone in his sexy blue eyes. 'About six. To start with.'

'Is that so?' Laughing, her heart swelling with love, she pushed him on to his back and wriggled provocatively on top of him, a mix of contentment and excited anticipation stirring through her as his arms closed round her, holding her close. 'Then I guess we'd better get started and not waste any more time.'

'My sentiments exactly.'

As Kyle looked into the face of the woman he loved more than life itself, a desperate ache of longing tightened inside him at the love and passion in Lexie's eyes. He drew her down, meeting the hot intensity of her kiss, revelling in the magic between them, unleashing the rage of desire that only seemed to burn ever hotter each time they were together.

Lexie had rescued him from the darkness of his past and had brought him into the light. She had freed him to be himself, had accepted him for who and what he was, and loved him anyway. It was the most liberating feeling. She had awakened and welcomed his own needs, matched and returned the depth of his desire, was his equal, his friend, his confidant, his lover.

As their passion flared and their bodies came together once more, Kyle gave himself up to the magic of making love with Lexie, the explosive pleasure they found together, the sensation of being part of her, one with her. They hurtled together towards oblivion, two souls inseparable, two hearts united, two lives entwined.

He couldn't wait to share the news of his joy with his special friends, Conor and Kate, Nic and Hannah, who each had found the specialness that he and Alexandra now experienced. His Lexie—the most loving and giving person he had ever known. By some miracle this amazing, wonderful woman wanted to give her love to him, and it was a gift he would treasure for the rest of their lives as they worked, lived, laughed and loved side by side.

In Lexie's loving care he was safe, as she was in his…now and for ever.

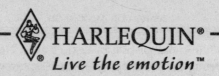

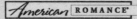

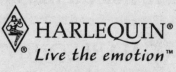

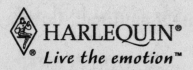

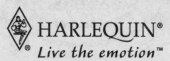